UNTAINTED LOVE

MEL DAU

Mel Dau Publications

Dedications

To every person who is silently suffering, this is for you.
You are worth it, and love is yours to conquer.

FROM MEL DAU:

Acknowledgements

Daddy,
Look what I did! Mel Dau Publications! You told me if I
dream it and put in the work, I can have it. I've been blessed
heavily in less than four months with my new publisher and
being able to get my rights to republish all my books. I'm
growing daily with amazing leadership and wonderful pen
sisters and brothers.

One

A va Mae Boyd

My team and I had busted our butts on this marketing presentation for the last six months. The time had come to show proof that this was what was best for the direction we wanted to take our branding campaign. I just finished the presentation with all the other executive leaders of the firm, and from the smile on their faces, I knew my team had this in the bag. I looked at my best friend and cousin, Myah, who is the Executive Director of Human Resources for our firm, and she looked to have stars in her eyes.

I am the Executive Director of Marketing for one of the leading financial firms in the world. At thirty-three years old, I worked extremely hard to be exactly where I am right now. After four years of undergraduate studies at South Carolina State University, I earned my bachelor's in marketing. I returned to my hometown of Charlotte, North Carolina, to complete my master's degree at the University of North Carolina, Charlotte. I was successful in my endeavors, receiving a Master of Science in Economics and Business Administration with a concentration in Applied Economics and Finance. My education and application thereof made me a secret weapon for any company, and they all knew it. I had job offers before I even graduated, but I started here with my current firm as a Junior Marketing Coordinator.

That was in 2010, and now, seven years later, I had aggressively worked my way up the ladder to Executive Director. Let me tell you, for a black woman, that was not an easy feat. My marketing strategies had brought this company multimillions, and my portfolio spoke for itself. As I stood in front of all the other executive directors of the firm, I knew that they knew my presentation was another golden check.

"Ms. Boyd, this presentation is flawless, and it is evident that your team has worked tirelessly on it. All I can smell is the money from this campaign." Mr. Chambers, the President, was so excited his face was a tinted red.

I smiled and thanked the room, then took my seat next to Myah. She grabbed my hand under the table as a job well done. The president and other executives spoke for about twenty more minutes, and after the green light was given to launch the campaign with the timeline I suggested, the meeting was adjourned.

Walking into Myah's office, we allowed the door to fully close before we started jumping and screaming with our signature wiggle, wiggle, shake, shake, booty pop, twerk, wiggle celebratory dance. We decided to do this in her office because her office was soundproof. We could get as loud as we wanted, and I loved it.

Myah kicked her shoes off and sat in her desk chair. "Girl, you gave them all of that black girl unicorn magic today! I knew they were in trouble when I saw that outfit you had on earlier this morning."

I laughed at her as I looked down at my outfit. I was a

beautiful girl, if I must say so myself. My toasted almond skin was the perfect sun-kissed color, and my eyes were a seductive dark brown. I had a head full of healthy hair that hit my upper back, but I often wore weaves. The maintenance is easier. At five-feet-seven inches tall, I was a thick girl wearing a size fourteen. My plump derriere looked amazing in my high-waisted black pencil skirt with my ruffled turtleneck collared white blouse. A simple broach was all I needed to complete the look with a fabulous pair of heels. I came in today to play ball, and I knocked it out the park.

"Girl, you already know I don't play when it comes to these marketing campaigns. My team worked so hard, and I can't wait to tell them the good news tonight at dinner." I sat on the couch in her office.

I was so confident in the work that my team did that I set up a celebratory dinner. I got every person on my team a gift for their hard work. I loved my team, and I took great pride in being a leader for them. I had worked in every position in the marketing line of business here at the firm, so I knew the struggles in each to better relate to my team.

"Ava Mae, you better be packed to leave in the morning, heifer. You know we have to be at the airport at five. I'm not playing with you." We were leaving in the morning for our girls' trip, and I was so excited because we were going to the Maldives. I have always wanted to stay at one of the water resorts where the bungalows are over the water. A whole week in paradise, I needed it.

"I'm going to be ready! The dinner starts at seven, and we'll be done by nine at the latest." I was annoyed that she called me by my first and middle name.

Myah has been doing that since she was a little girl. We grew up down the block from each other in Shannon Park. Our fathers are brothers, and both of our parents still live in the houses we grew up in. Myah was a year older than me, but because of an early birthday, we were always in the same grade. She's been my best friend from the sandbox and has been with me through thick and thin. We talked for a little longer before I left to complete some work and set out my delegation assignments while I was out for the week. My team was going to be so happy to hear our campaign had been accepted, and we were moving forward.

❦

IT WAS THREE-THIRTY IN THE MORNING, AND I WAS exhausted, but I knew I was gonna sleep my ass off on this plane since it took thirty-six hours to get there. Those ticket prices almost took me out, but of course, Myah reminded me of my yearly salary and investment portfolio. Myah lives in Ballantyne, so she should be on her way here to pick me up. Hopefully, Anthony, her husband, doesn't hold her up. She's always late because he "holds her up". When Myah arrived at a quarter after four, I already knew what it was when I saw the red mark on her neck.

"We should have just met at the airport. I knew Anthony wasn't going to let you out of the house easily." I chuckled at the look she gave me.

"Don't try my husband." She paused and smacked her lips, making me laugh. "For your information, he's going on a boys' trip with his homeboy, Isaac. That's the only reason he was up; their flight leaves around the same time ours does."

"Where is he going?" She looked off for a second before she spoke.

"Damn, I totally forgot to ask. Ugh, he knows I get discombobulated when he gives me the D."

I couldn't help but laugh at her because she stayed being discombobulated after her husband's D. She said she would call him when we got to the airport and were checked in. I thought we should have just taken an Uber to the airport, but Myah didn't want to be bothered. I couldn't believe this flight was thirty-six hours. I'm about to sleep so good on this plane. The price of these first-class tickets was a semester in college, I swear. I was going to drink and be merry. TSA Pre-check was created by God because it moved so much faster, and we were done in no time.

"I'm going to sleep so good on this plane," Myah said as we walked to our gate. I was on the same wavelength, so all I did was nod my head.

We got to our gate and settled in since our flight was still about thirty minutes away from boarding. I felt like I was going to fall asleep right there in the waiting area. I thought about the previous night and the excitement of my team when I delivered the news of our campaign being picked up. We ended up having drinks and not leaving until about eleven-thirty. That was completely not in the plan, but I figured it would be OK since this flight took forever. We were leaving on a Thursday and returning a little over a week later, next Friday. I decided to rest my eyes for a minute while we waited for our flight to board, hoping I didn't fully fall asleep.

"Oh, *hell* no!" Myah's loud voice jarred me from my light slumber, and I jumped in my seat at the unknown. As my eyes focused, all I could do was laugh at the sight in front of me. This was going to be interesting.

Two

M yah Boyd Montgomery

I WAS SO READY TO GO ON THIS GIRLS' TRIP WITH AVA. IT was our twice-a-year ritual to go on a trip in the country and one out of the country. We alternated who picked the location, and I picked the location this time because I knew Ava wanted to stay in an overwater bungalow. It was a pricey trip, I will admit, but we both could definitely afford it. Ava and I were bosses at our firm; in fact, we were the only two Executive Directors that were African American women. We demanded the respect of our counterparts, and it was given because our work spoke for itself.

I attended South Carolina State University, obtaining a bachelor's in communications. We both graduated top of our classes with her being the valedictorian and myself as the salutatorian. Everyone at State referred to us as the "Boyd Girls". After graduation, we both returned to Charlotte, North Carolina, and I decided to pursue my master's at

Phoenix University in Human Resource Management. I took the first offer I got after graduation with a local staffing firm as a recruiter coordinator. That's where I met my fine ass husband, Anthony Montgomery. He submitted an application for placement, and we had a position for him in a plant. I was the one who coordinated all of his interviews and things, but unfortunately, he didn't get the job because of a felony charge he had on his record, dealing with drugs.

We ran into each other again a couple of months later at a sport's bar where we both were rooting for Carolina and hit it off. The rest is pretty much history. Anthony is sexy with his light skin and kaleidoscope eyes. He was taller than my five-feet-five height, standing at six-feet-one, but I loved the climb. Anthony wore his hair in a small afro and rocked a goatee. Man, he was so sexy, and people often compared him to Michael Ealy. Our relationship had its ups and downs, but once we got his laundry mat business off the ground, it was a lot better. I figured since it was hard for him to get a job under someone else, he should work for himself. That was in 2008, and now we own a chain of laundry mats. We married in 2011 in an amazing outdoor wedding in the park.

This morning when I woke up, Anthony was already up, and I knew it was about to be some mess because he isn't a morning person. He let me know that since I was leaving him, he went ahead and planned a boys' trip with his home-boy, Isaac. I thought that was cool, so we could have away time at the same time and not really miss each other. He, of course, wouldn't let me leave out of the house without dipping into my honeypot, but I didn't mind one bit. He told me his flight left around the same time ours did, but I never thought to ask this man where he was going. I needed someone to explain to me why my husband and Isaac were standing in front of me with carryon bags and a damn smirk.

"Tony! What in the ham and cheese sammich are you doing here? Oh, you stopped at our gate on the way to yours?" I asked with my hands on my thick hips, and I heard Ava giggling behind me.

I was a thick girl at a size sixteen, but I was solid, and my husband loved every inch of me. People often told me I resembled Tabria Majors, and I took that as a big compliment. That girl is gorgeous. When I first met my husband, I wasn't sure about dating him, because hell, we both light-skinned for all intent and purposes. I was used to dating dark-skinned dudes, but his personality won me over. He had a street edge, but he handles his business. I respected him because he could have let the system take him under, but a high school diploma gave him the keys to becoming a very successful business owner. Between our business, investments, and my job, we didn't have any financial worries.

"What you mean? I told you I was going on a boys' trip." His little smirk as he talked annoyed me, and I moved closer to him. He immediately enveloped me in his arms.

"Tony, don't play. Where are you going? Is your gate down this way?" I looked in his eyes as I asked the questions. I looked over at Isaac, and he gave me an innocent shrug, then moved to sit in the seat near Ava. Ava just looked and smiled at him, but I knew she thought he was fine as wine. When I first met him, I almost wanted to swap dudes. They grew up together in Hidden Valley and ran the streets together.

Anthony kissed me on my neck before he told me exactly what I didn't want to hear. "Nah, this is my gate. We going to the Maldives. You know they have overwater bungalows?"

Hell no! I threw my hands up in frustration, which caused Anthony to chortle at my antics. This man *knew* we were going to the Maldives. I had been talking about this trip for almost eight months, now he wants to tell me he just so happens to be going to the same location. I moved away from my husband and looked between him, Isaac, and Ava. They all were laughing at this point.

"Really, Anthony? You just so happen to decide to come to the Maldives the same time I was going on my girls' trip?" He was still thinking all of this was comical, but I had a little trick for his yellow ass. He gon' learn today.

"You know what, that's cool. See if I talk to you on this trip. Got me messed up." I was more annoyed than mad. I plopped down in my seat next to Ava, and she placed her hand on my leg. When I looked at her, she was smiling.

"Pudge, why are you so mad? You know how he is. Hell, I'm surprised he didn't beat us there to surprise you on the beach," she stated in a light manner. I knew she was trying to help me not want to choke this man out, but I wasn't sure if it was working just yet.

I knew she was right, but I didn't care. He thought this was all too funny as he sat next to me and kissed my neck. I had something for him, just wait 'til we get to our destination. I hope their asses are flying economy, too.

৩৯৩

FOR THIRTY-SIX-HOURS, I SAT MY ASS IN MY FIRST-CLASS pod and *tried* to ignore Anthony. It was kind of hard when they bought the pods next to us. I swear this man gets on my nerves. It's like he looked at my trip information and booked everything I did. He tried to get me to get nasty in the bathroom so we could join the mile-high club, but I declined, begrudgingly. I was trying really hard to stay mad, but he is so fine, and the D is so amazingly perfect. The way he grabs my thick hips when he hits it from the back... *No!* I will not think about it, or he will have me bent over in this plane's bathroom.

Ava thinks this whole situation is cute and funny, but she

won't be laughing anymore when Isaac is on that ass. Isaac has wanted to talk to Ava for as long as I have known him. When they met at my and Anthony's wedding, Ava was married. Now that she's not, she has totally closed herself off to love, and I hate that. Isaac, or Solomon, as we mainly call him, is a good man, fine as fuck, too, but don't tell my husband I said that.

When we finally arrived in the Maldives, Ava was almost on the floor laughing because I was trying to beat them off the plane. I refused to ride anywhere together, but I see my loving husband thought of everything.

The car service I ordered was told there was a change in plans, and they were now here in a Tahoe to escort all of us to our resort. The smirk on Anthony's face made me want to smack it off, but I had something even better. Getting to our resort, I was lost in the beauty. Ava and I jumped around like little girls in excitement as we walked to the check-in desk. We were greeted by the front desk receptionist.

"Hi, Myah Montgomery checking in with Ava Boyd." I was so excited, and my pockets were about to be, too. When the receptionist asked for the card I wanted on file for incidentals, I turned around and gave my husband that same smirk.

"Mr. Montgomery, can I have your black card, please?" I used my sweetest tone and wanted to laugh at his facial expression.

He crossed his arms over his chest and tilted his head before responding. "Why do you need my card? This your trip."

Placing my hand on my hips, I gave him a reminder. "I want your card because you told me that whenever I am in your presence, I would never have to go into my pockets. Since you want to be here with me, hubby, run her your card."

I stepped to the side and Ava busted out laughing. Isaac was looking at the events, shaking his head with a chuckle. "She got you there, my dude. Go ahead and run her that card."

Anthony moved to me and placed his mouth at my ear. "I see what you doing, My, but just remember this when I'm in that pussy later."

With a hard smack on my butt, he walked over and gave her the card for our bungalows, the one Ava and I would be in as well as his and Isaac's. Shortly after, we headed to our bungalows, and they were amazing! The one that we were in was like a two-bedroom apartment with a full kitchen and living area. The bathroom was one right out of a magazine. Walking out of the patio door, you were met by the gorgeous, clear waters of the Indian Ocean. I wanted to live here forever. Looking to my left side, I immediately got annoyed. How the hell did this man pull off getting the bungalow directly next to ours?

"My! Ain't this beautiful? Damn, we shoulda been came here, bae!" I looked at this man like he had bumped his damn head. *We* didn't come anywhere! I didn't even respond as I walked back into our bungalow to see what Ava was doing.

I loved my cousin and her resilience. She had been through so much and held her head high every day. What would kill most pushed her to be even greater.

"Ava, what you doing in here?" She was in the kitchen, looking in the cabinets. Ava's ass could eat! I swear, I love her for it too because she is always down to meet me at three in the morning for a midnight diner run or something. Before we got to the resort, they asked if there were any grocery items that we wanted to request for the room. I sent these folks a long list and I was happy to see that everything I requested was there.

"Girl, these folks got all my favorites in here! I love this place! They're going to mess around and have me tell them I'm working remotely and stay a week longer." Ava turned as she spoke, placing a potato chip in her mouth.

"Girl, you know I'm always down! Glad we both brought our work laptops. At least that way, we can get a true girls' trip." My remark was said with a huff.

"The hell you say! You stay an extra week, we staying an extra week. Don't get handled in here, my nigga."

What the! Hearing Anthony's voice, I threw my hands up. Turning to see him and Isaac standing in our living room had me over him.

"How are you in here right now, Anthony? Please tell me you are not going to annoy me the whole trip," I exclaimed as I stood with my arms across my chest. Anthony laughed and came into my space, like it was his.

Kissing my lips, Anthony smacked my ass. "You know if I'm paying for a room, I'm going to have a key, My. Stop acting like you don't know me."

Isaac busted out laughing, which made me look at him like he had two heads. Looking at Ava, she was too busy eating chips with a smirk and eyeing Isaac. All I could do was laugh at him because, as much as I was annoyed, I was turned on by my husband's desire to be in my space. When I first told him about our trip, I knew he was going to tell me hell no, but he didn't. I should have known right then and there that he was up to some BS. Since being with Anthony, we had never spent more than two consecutive days away from each other, so I don't know why I would think he would let me be gone for a week.

I moved to speak in my babe's ear so only he could hear. "I do know you and it's because of that very reason that I have the urge to give you the best head of your life right now."

The smirk that covered his face let me know he was down, like he always was.

"Aye, we'll be right back," Anthony told Ava and Isaac before pulling me out of our bungalow into his.

My husband stayed ready for this mouth.

Three

I saac Solomon Mills

MY DUDE ANTHONY WAS A WILD DUDE. WHEN HE CAME TO me months ago about this trip, I was hesitant because he told me her cousin Ava was coming. Also, I remembered she was married, but apparently not anymore. Ava was fine as hell, always had been. I met her at Anthony's wedding, but like I said, she was married. I don't fuck with women who are in relationships, situationships, or anything like that. I had a short temper at times, and I had too much to lose. A dude got one time to step to me over some female and someone was going to not leave the situation alive. Oh, I always leave alive.

I grew up in Hidden Valley, pretty much since my family moved here from Charleston, South Carolina, when I was twelve. Anthony was one of the first dudes I met when I was getting jumped by some dumb asses and Anthony was the only one that jumped in to help me. We handled the four dudes with little effort, and from that point on, it was us against the world. We jumped off the porch together, partied together and even went up the road together. I was happy for my dude when he met Myah. He needed someone to even keel him and she was it. When I saw Ava the first time at their wedding, I wanted her but she appeared to be happily dancing with her husband, so I let the thought leave my mind.

Over the years, I had been too busy building an empire to even think of her or any female for that matter. Don't get me wrong, I get my dick wet, but as far as a relationship, I don't have time. If it's worth it, yeah, but other than that, nah, I'm good. I am the owner and sole proprietor of Mills Vending Services. My company supplies and stocks vending machines throughout Charlotte. We have hot and cold machines and because of our wide selection of products from organic to junk food, we have cornered the market. I currently have contracts with the school district in Charlotte and Union County as well as two healthcare systems in Charlotte. I employ over one hundred people currently. I was proud of my accomplishments because all I knew was the streets, so finding something to get me out was a big deal. I was proud of Anthony as well with his laundry mat chain and, of course, my machines were in all of them.

I had no idea Myah didn't know we were coming on this trip and her reaction to it was hilarious. They were like the perfect match. Seeing Ava at the airport was a sight for sore eyes because she was gorgeous. Her smooth skin looked baby soft and I wanted to touch it. I wasn't sure if she was wearing a weave or not, but I didn't really care. The shit was sexy. I spoke to her when I sat down and she spoke back, but it was in a shy manner. I was going to try and break her out of her shell on this trip. I didn't think I was an intimidating person to feel shy around, but maybe she was a shy person. I didn't know much about her, but I was going to get to know as much as I could.

The Maldives was gorgeous, and I knew I would be back again, hopefully with a boo. Standing in Ava and Myah's bungalow with Ava after Anthony snatched Myah up out of here, I felt nervous. She was so damn beautiful standing in the kitchen, leaning on the counter, eating a bag of chips. She was tearing them damn chips up, too.

"Damn, Ma, can I have some?" I walked towards her as I voiced my request. She looked up from the bag as if she just realized I was still in the room. Her brown face took a reddish tint from her blushing and it was cute. She extended the opened bag in my direction, and I accepted the offering. I see why she was tearing these chips up; salt and pepper chips are the shit.

"So, you excited to spend the week here? You ever been here before?" I ate some more chips, waiting for her answer.

She shifted on her feet before looking into my eyes, and I swear I saw our future babies and grandbabies. "No, I haven't, but I am so excited. All I want to do is lay on the beach and read or on the patio. Have you been out there?"

Her face lit up as she spoke... I wanted to give her ass the world. Damn, this might be her. My mother always told me there would be a girl that would have the ability to snatch your soul just by looking at you. Well, Ava Boyd has my soul and she doesn't even know it.

"Nah, show me." I wanted to see outside, but more so, I wanted to see that ass in those shorts she was wearing. I'm still a man.

Ava walked past me and I got a nice look at her thick ass. It was shaking like hell in those shorts. The shorts weren't even short, but damn. Walking onto their patio, I was immediately drawn into the beauty of the world around us. This is the first time I had ever been out of the country; hell, I just got my passport. Anthony told me Myah and Ava go out of the country somewhere different every year. I'm going to have to get out more often because this shit was gorgeous.

"Damn, this shit is amazing." I was in awe and didn't really know what to say. I was standing directly behind Ava and between the view and her natural scent, I was at a loss for words.

When Ava stepped back, she bumped into me and my hands automatically went to her hips. Feeling her breath hitch, I let her go, but I damn sure didn't want to. "My bad, Ma. I didn't mean to be right up on you."

I stepped to the side and she turned to look at me. Those blushing cheeks would be the death of me. She looked down at her feet, and on instinct, I lifted her head with my fingers under her chin.

"You're too beautiful to look down, Ma. Always hold your head up." I felt compelled to tell her that. She was too fucking gorgeous to ever hold her head down for anything. Her smile was so warm it would lighten a dark night.

"Thank you, Isaac, or do you want me to call you Solomon?" Her voice was so soft in this moment. She could call me *got* because she damn sure got me wanting to bend her ass over.

"You can call me whatever you want to."

She gave a smirk to my response. "What does everyone call you?"

"Most people call me Solomon." She placed one of her hands on her hip, drawing my eyes to it. When she popped it, I knew she was gonna be mine – fuck that.

"Well, I'm special, so I'm going to call you Isaac or Mills." She winked at the end of her statement and walked around me, back into the bungalow. She damn sure is special.

AFTER MYAH AND ANTHONY FINISHED DOING WHATEVER they were doing, we all decided to go to the beach. Of course, we got to the beach before the girls. I don't know how long it takes to put on a bathing suit, but apparently, an hour or more. This resort was lit as hell and I was happy it was all-inclusive. For the price we had to pay, it better had been or I was cursing someone the fuck out. I like keeping my money.

"My dude, I see you looking at Ava. What's up with that?" Sitting in the cabana, I looked over at my best friend and just gave him a smirk. He knew what that meant. "Nigga, Ava not gon' give you no play, trust. I've tried to hook little sis up multiple times and she leave them panting. I'm telling you; I half think she's a damn lesbian."

My outburst of laughter was hard and loud. "Trust me, the way her body reacted to my touch, she's not a lesbian. Well, what happened with her husband? I remember dude; he was a cool cat from what I remember."

Anthony looked off for a beat, then looked back at me. "Man, he died like five years ago. Shit was sad as fuck. She doesn't really talk about it, but she loved that man. She went into a deep ass depression after that. I remember times Myah would stay with her for days, especially after she attempted suicide. I've never seen my wife so helpless and distraught. Ever since then, she just not here for no new niggas."

Anthony spoke in a daze as if he was in that moment. I didn't know all that, and I knew if I wanted her, I would have to be slow and patient. "Damn, man. Well, I kinda understand, Ma. It's hard to get over a lost love. I'm gonna make something shake, though."

We sipped on our alcoholic drinks and smoked a blunt. From my side view, I saw the girls coming down the beach. Turning my full attention to them, I had to grab myself to calm the beast. Ava had on this black two-piece bathing suit with some net dress thing over it. Did I say Ava was slim thick? Looks like she was a size twelve or more. I'm not a fan of skinny girls, so she was just right, and I knew if I ever got her pregnant, her ass would be even thicker.

"Myah gon' make me kick her ass on this beach." Anthony's voice broke my thoughts and I chuckled. He was always with the shits when it came to her.

"Bruh, why you trippin'? You here with her."

Anthony stood to his feet and looked down at me. "Man, she didn't know we were coming when she packed that little shit. That means she had plans to be ass out while I wasn't here."

He didn't wait another second before he made his way to her. From the look on her face, she knew she had a problem. All I could do was shake my head at them and return my gaze to Ava's sexy ass. The closer she got to me, the bigger my smile got. Damn, I want this girl. She sat in the seat next to me and all I could do was look at her.

"You look sexy as hell, Ma. Damn." Her signature blushing tone took over her face.

"Thank you, Isaac."

I wanted to get to know her a little bit, so I started my questions. It was a smooth conversation and I was impressed because she was definitely a boss chick, but I shouldn't be surprised. Myah doesn't hang with the subpar types. She had a corny sense of humor, but it was funny on her. She laughed at her own jokes before anyone else could. I thought it was cute. I didn't want to bring up her husband, but I kinda wanted to see where her head was at.

"So, if I remember correctly, you were married. What happened with that?" I knew I was taking a risk changing the entire mood by asking her this, but I needed to see if she was really one hundred percent closed to anything new.

Her smile fell and she looked off into the ocean. Without looking at me, she said in a monotone, "My husband died some years back. I don't really like to talk about it. I loved, I lost, life goes on."

I stayed silent for a beat to give her time to breathe, then I spoke. "My condolences. I'm sorry for bringing it up. I didn't know, Ma."

She nodded her head in acknowledgement but didn't look at me. I reached out and touched her leg to get her attention. She looked at me with sad eyes.

"Hey, come back to me. We not there anymore; smile for me, beautiful." She wiped the single tear that escaped from her eyes and gave me a weak smile. I don't know what it is about her, but I just wanted to take her pain away.

Four

A^{va}

DEAR, GOD, WHY WOULD YOU DO THIS TO ME? HAVE ME ON this gorgeous beach with a man that looks like he was made perfect in Your sight. I know this is probably the wrong thing to say to you, being God and all, but I want to bust it open and bring it back. Sit and spin on it until I have his little chocolate babies. His chocolate skin and those dreads, Jesus be a panty liner.

When my eyes landed on Isaac in the airport, I had to clench my legs closed because that man was everything. I don't know if he wears oils or something, but if you were told to bottle sexy, it would be whatever he was wearing. He was definitely making me nervous. His beard seemed like it was calling out for me to pull it. I knew I would have to stay far away from him, and I thought I was doing good until we went out on the patio. I felt him behind me, I did, but when I stepped back and his hand grabbed my waist, everything I thought I knew, I forgot.

The bathing suit I decided to wear was a Fashion Nova fit

and I was a little self-conscious but Myah told me to shut the hell up. Rude Heifer. I loved Myah's confidence. When we were younger, she was teased because she was a heavy kid all the way up until college. She lost over one hundred pounds in college and it was on. Even when she was heavier, she could still take your man. If you got a smart mouth about it, she would take your lunch, too. When you're around her, your confidence has to step up or move over, period.

I really enjoyed talking to Isaac. He's a good listener and he laughs at my jokes. Everyone always tells me my jokes are corny, but I get the last laugh because fine ass Isaac thinks I'm funny. I was really enjoying our time, but a cloud of sadness hovered over me, knowing I couldn't go any further with this. I just wasn't ready or able. I also wasn't ready or able to think or talk about my late husband Andre. His death was too painful, and I tried every day to block it out of my head. I loved Andre with my whole heart, mind, and soul so losing him was detrimental to my life.

"Hey, come back to me. We not there anymore; smile for me, beautiful." Hearing Isaac's soothing voice and feeling his touch brought me out of my haze. I wiped my lone tear and gave him a smile. Looking out into the water, I smiled at Myah and Anthony having the time of their lives. He was her perfect match and I loved that for my cousin.

Isaac stood from his seat and extended his hand. "Come on, we can't let them have all the fun."

I placed my hand in his and allowed him to pull me from the chair. I came on vacation to have fun, not be sad and think about my past. As we walked to the water, he challenged me to a race and my response to that was to take off running. I ran as fast as I could while I laughed, but I messed up when I turned to see how far ahead I was. He was right on me and he grabbed me, tossing me over his shoulder. God, I loved his touch.

"You better not drop me, Isaac!" He was running fast with me over his shoulder. Let me tell you, the way this man's body is set up, I wanted to lick every tattoo.

"Hope you didn't plan to keep your hair dry." Isaac's statement made me scream right before he dunked both of us in the water.

He's lucky I know how to swim, but for the sake of being able to hold on to him a little longer, I feigned ignorance to any swimming ability. When we rose out of the water, I was laughing and so was he. I stood on my feet and tried to push him under, but he was too strong... I was in his arms once again.

"Aww, look at the two love birds." Hearing Myah brought me back to reality and I let Isaac go. The look of confusion he gave me was understandable because we were just having fun. I didn't mind having fun, but I didn't want to lead him on because I knew nothing would ever come of this.

"Shut up, Myah." I stepped away from Isaac towards Myah. I already knew what she was thinking before she said it and I hope she didn't.

"Aye, let's play a game or some shit," Anthony suggested and we all agreed.

We spent the next couple of hours, playing various water games and having fun. Isaac was so fun to be around and it's like every time he touched me, I felt alive. By the time we left the beach to head back to the bungalows, I was tipsy and hungry. We separated while we prepped for dinner.

After getting out of the shower, I relaxed for a second on the patio to air dry. I had on undies, but I left my top off. I turned on my stomach because I remembered that Myah's husband was next door. I didn't want any problems. The sun was setting, so there was a slight breeze off the water, and I loved it. I could sleep out here all night. I must have dozed off because feeling my shoulder being shaken startled me. Looking up, I saw a dressed Myah.

"Girl, get your behind up so you can get ready to go. The guys are supposed to be here in like forty-five minutes." She stayed fussing.

"Why you let me fall asleep? I was just trying to air dry." I got up and wrapped myself in my towel to walk inside. Myah was on my heels.

"So, Anthony said Isaac wants to see what's popping. He's fine as wine, isn't he?" I was moisturizing my body, listening to her go on and on about Isaac. She does this often about different men she thinks I should date. I wish she would just stop already.

"Myah, why do you do this? You know just like I know, I'm not interested. I'm good." I had pulled out my clothes before I took my shower, so it took me no time to put on my dress.

Hearing Myah huff, I knew I was about to get a damn lecture and I wasn't wrong.

"Ava, why do you do this to yourself? You deserve to be happy and there is no reason that you can't, and you know that. You are just being stubborn and allowing yourself to wallow in something that you don't have to anymore. Ava, how long has it been?"

Turning around to look at her after I finished dressing, I crossed my arms over my chest. "It doesn't matter how long it has been. I'm not ready, and I probably never will be." The more I talked, the more irritated I got. "Why is that so hard to believe? I'm fine! I have my career and I live a good damn life, Myah." My voice raised, and I made sure to enunciate each word when I added, "I don't need a man!"

I was so over this damn conversation and was happy when I heard the guys entering our bungalow. Walking out of my room, I stopped dead in my tracks when I saw Isaac.

Damn. This man was standing before me in a pair of burgundy slacks that fit him to perfection with a white-collar shirt with the sleeves rolled up. The shirt showed how cut he was, and with the sleeves rolled up, his tattoo sleeves were on display. His dreads were pulled back and beard was lined to perfection. Looking at his feet, he had on loafers, and I love a man in loafers. *Jesus, why are You testing me?*

Isaac walked into my personal space and his cologne had me tightening my legs together.

"Ma, you look beautiful. That dress might get you in trouble tonight."

I gave him a slight smile and let him know I had to grab my clutch. I was disappointed because, in any other situation, I would have jumped on Isaac, but I just wasn't ready. I was annoyed with it all. Myah came in the room and stood in the door, looking at me.

"What, Myah?" I was annoyed being under her stare.

"So, you going to look at all that chocolate out there and let it pass you by because you're scared? You're a fool, Ava." She didn't even wait for me to curse her out. She just left the same way she came. At this point, I was ready to get this dinner over with and go the hell to bed.

৩%৪

DINNER WAS AMAZING, EVEN WITH MY INITIAL ATTITUDE. I really enjoyed everyone's company, especially Isaac. The couple glasses of wine didn't help; well, more like five glasses and two mixed drinks. I'm not going to say I'm drunk, but I feel pleasantly happy. Walking back to the bungalows, I knew Myah's ass was going to be laying up with her husband. She was all over him on this walk back, all I could do was shake my head. Looking over at Isaac, I wanted to jump his damn bones and clearly that took precedence over watching where the hell I was going.

"Whoa, watch yaself, lil' mama." Isaac broke my fall. Damn, let me get in this room.

"Thank you." I gathered myself as he held me around my waist as we walked to the bungalow.

"Ava, you mind if I crash on ya couch? It looks like Mya and Anthony have some plans that I would rather not hear. Not sure if you know, but they can get loud as hell."

I couldn't contain my laughter because I knew he was right. They were loud as hell and didn't care who was around.

"Yea, you don't have to sleep on couch, just sleep in Myah's bed." He nodded his head to my instruction as we entered my bungalow. Telling him goodnight, I hurried to my room before doing something I regret. After taking off my clothes and washing my face, it took no time for me to fall asleep once my head it the pillow. I hoped I'd dream about Isaac.

Waking up in a cold sweat was not how I wanted to spend any of my time on this vacation. Looking over at the clock, noticing it was three o'clock in the morning, I just wanted to go to sleep. Since Andre died, this happened sometimes and Myah always laid with me. I love her for that because she lives in Ballantyne and I live in a condo Uptown, but she never says no. Getting out of my bed, I stretched then headed to Myah's room to get in bed with her. Looking out of the patio door on my way to her room, I admired the full moon's reflection off of the water. I just love it here.

Myah's room was dark, so I moved cautiously. Our rooms had the same layout but in the opposite direction. Getting to the bed, I pulled the covers back and climbed in. I immediately felt comfort just knowing I wasn't alone anymore. My sleep immediately began to overtake me, and when she wrapped her arms around me, sleep found me effortlessly.

Five

Isaac

AVA IS CONFUSING AS HELL, MAN. IT'S LIKE SHE'S FEELING me then, all of a sudden, she blocks herself. I really don't get it. Understand, I'm a good-looking nigga, period. I keep my body tight because I go to the gym often and sometimes when my workers have things going on, I cover shifts. There is a lot of manual lifting in certain parts of my company. My locs look like God himself twists them, but my mom does. She had been doing my hair since I was a kid; no one else will touch my hair. I don't even let females play in my hair. She actually shaped me up too since she's a hairstylist and master barber. I admire my mother because she was doing the barber thing when it wasn't popular for females to be doing it. My father is a barber as well, that's how they met. I'm a black ass man but I love it and so do the ladies.

I'm really feeling Ava's little thick ass. Well, she isn't that little, standing at what looks like, maybe five-feet-seven but that was nothing for my six-feet-three height. I loved when she had to look up at me... and those lips. *Bruh*! I want to kiss them so bad, but she was so hot and cold with me.

Like at the beach, it was cool, but it's almost like she would let herself go then realize she's doing it and catch herself. That's why I'm confused as fuck, hearing her come in my room for tonight. I'm a night owl so I rarely fall asleep 'til about four or five in the morning and then sleep until about eleven in the morning. Being your own boss has its perks.

I heard her come in my room, and since my eyes had already adjusted to the darkness, plus the moonlight gave the room some illumination, I was able to see she only had on a t-shirt. She climbed in the bed and I was frozen for a minute. What the hell she on? I thought about it and took a chance when I wrapped my arm around her. There was a sudden peace, and I felt sleep coming earlier than normal. Feeling her relax in my arms made me relax and I welcomed sleep.

⚜

"LET ME FIND THE HELL OUT!" HEARING MYAH'S LOUD mouth made me jump out of my sleep. I still had Ava in my arms and was sleeping good as hell. I can't remember ever sleeping with a chick. I mean, I pipe these bitches and send them on their merry way. Holding Ava in my arms felt so damn right. Looking to the room door, Myah and Anthony were both looking at us in shock. I didn't understand why, we were just sleeping. Feeling Ava move in my arms, I loosened my hold on her and she snuggled her face into my neck. Her breath on my neck was stinky but still felt good. When I felt her body stiffen in my arms, I figured she realized she was in the bed with me. My thoughts were confirmed when she pulled her face from my neck and looked at me in horror.

"Oh my God! What did I do?" Her voice had so much fear and I didn't understand. The way and speed at which she jumped out of the bed, you would think I was a rapist or some shit, and I didn't appreciate that.

"Ma. We ain't do shit. You came in here with me," I let her know off gate because she was not about to handle me like I did something wrong. Her little ass came a room over and got in bed with me.

She wrapped herself in her arms and made eye contact with me. In the softest and most innocent voice, she asked, "We didn't have sex?"

I walked around the bed towards her. Once I got close, I placed my hands on her arms before reassuring her. "No, Ma, we just slept. You felt good in my arms."

"Ah, shit now! Brother-in-law, you better shoot your shot." Myah's outburst made us all laugh.

"Shut up, My, and mind your damn business. We were coming to get y'all for breakfast." Anthony was trying to talk through his laughs. I took the time to look at Ava and she was looking at me and I could tell she was questioning herself, so I delivered a kiss to her forehead.

We parted ways and got ready to go to breakfast. Breakfast was as I expected. We had a lot of fun and enjoyed each other's company. The rest of the week held the same pattern. We had fun, and at some point, she would pull back. When we went parasailing, she was so scared that she held my hand the whole time, but as soon as we were done, she let it go like she was doing something wrong. I tried to rationalize her behavior and the only thing I could come up with was being scared or not wanting to move on from her husband. Maybe she thinks it's disrespectful to his memory to be with someone else.

WE HAD BEEN BACK FROM THE TRIP FOR A WEEK AND I couldn't stop thinking about Ava. I just didn't understand what it was about this damn girl. I had never been pressed for a chick before. Ever. I couldn't understand it. I needed to make the decision if I wanted to even pursue this any further. I know what I needed to do. There was always one place I went when I needed to get good advice from level heads. They never steered me wrong.

Walking into my mom and dad's shop, Vintage Styles & Cutz, I was greeted with the same love as I always am. My parents have owned this shop since before we even moved to Charlotte. It's had a couple different names but no other shop in the area could compete. My mom looks amazing for her age of fifty-four. Her and my pops had me when they were young. My mom was eighteen and my dad was twenty, but the love they have for each other is what I want.

"Hey, son! What's up withca?" My dad was cutting Antho-ny's head and I had to look at this man, like how you come to my people spot and not tell me?

"Nothing, Pops, where Mama?" I questioned as I hugged and dapped him up. I punched Anthony in the arm once I pulled back.

"Bruh, hit me again, and we squarin' up in here, and I don't care if Mama Lilli whoop me. I knew you was going to come here today. Heard it all in your voice this morning when you were talking about Ava not wanting you." Anthony smirked with his comment.

"Who don't want my baby? She's a fool. Leave her alone, son." Hearing my mama enter the shop from the other side where the hair salon was made me smile. I was the epitome of a Mama's Boy, but not to the point where it crippled me. She definitely made me stand up like a man and my father expected the same, if not more.

"Mama, you know everybody want the kid." I reminded as

I hugged her. "I just got a little dilemma with a female I'm feeling." I removed her from my arms. "Mama, I don't get her. It's like she likes me, but she stops herself from liking me when she realizes what she doing. We spent a week together when Anthony ambushed Myah's trip. She's Myah's cousin." I said all of that while hugging my mama and sitting in her chair for her to retwist my hair. She has a booth on both sides of the shop.

"Well, babe. Tell me about her."

I took the time to tell my mother and father, since his chair is right next to hers, about Ava. Anthony chimed in from time to time. My mom didn't interrupt me as I talked, and she never does. She is what I call an intensive listener; when she listens, she not only listens to your words, she listens to your tone and pays attention to your body language. After I finished talking, she didn't immediately reply. She looked at my father and it was as if they were having a silent conversation. It was always like that, as if they share one brain.

"Son, you have to be careful when you are handling a person who has suffered a great loss like a spouse. I'm sure based on what you said it still feels fresh for her. Five years is not a long time to settle in those feelings of loss," she said to me as I looked at her through the mirror while she retwisted my hair.

"I'm going to tell you something I never have and maybe from this you will have a better understanding of how she feels." I arched my brow at my mother before looking at my father, then Anthony. The shop wasn't packed at all, so it was pretty much just us for right now.

"As you know, I had you when I was eighteen, fresh out of high school. I was so happy to be your mother and have a baby for The Isaac Soloman Mills Senior. I loved your father just as fiercely back then as I do now. Well, I love him more now because back then, I was a young girl, and we went through a lot of unnecessary drama due to both of our immaturities. Anyway, we were married before you were one year old and shortly after your second birthday, I got pregnant again.

I was so excited and so was your father."

She paused and gave my father a loving look. He reached over and placed his hand behind her neck and pulled her to him. He gave her a kiss on her temple and rubbed her back, speaking into her ear. I always relished the way they loved each other. I wanted that and I would settle for nothing less.

I turned my seat in their direction so she could finish, but my father picked up where she left off. "We were pregnant and happy as hell, son. When we found out we were having a girl, I was going to shit a brick, but your mom was beaming. You know little girls have a way of wrapping you around their finger without even trying. Hell, your mama got me like that already, so to add another one, I was scared."

My father's light chuckle made my mother smile at the thought. "Everything was great until one day, when she was thirty-six weeks, we went for a checkup and there was no heartbeat. It's like nothing or no one could explain it. Our little girl was gone. The worst part is your mother had to deliver her as if she was alive. I will never forget the helplessness I felt as a man and a father watching her endure the pain of childbirth without the reward."

Damn, I never knew any of this. I felt bad for my mom and dad. My mother looked at me with sad eyes.

"Son, after that loss, I didn't want any more children. Your father did but I selfishly denied him that right because I felt having another baby was like replacing Angelica. That's what we named her. I denied your father and it almost tore our marriage apart." She looked at my father when she said that, and he kissed her lips in reassurance.

My father looked at me and spoke. "See, son, sometimes loss makes us make decisions that hurt and affect others we love. I forgave your mother a long time ago and we worked through it. It eventually brought us closer, but for Ava, she is still dealing with a fresh loss. She may like you very much but thinks by loving you, she is not loving her late husband, although one really has nothing to do with the other."

Looking at Anthony, he seemed to be in deep thought as well. It was a lot to think about, but it did give me insight into how Ava may be feeling. I was still very conflicted because I really liked her. Usually, I would just write a chick off, but I felt in my heart this was not a situation that I should.

"Ma, I don't know what to say. Like damn, I'm sorry you had to go through that, and it does help me kinda understand what Ava might be going through. But... Ma. I still really like her. There's something about her that I can't let go." I had to be honest about the situation.

My mother took her place back behind me and hugged me from the back. "Then you pursue her heart, son, but do it carefully. When you get her, love her fiercely and without reservation because I can guarantee she's worth it."

That's exactly what I would do. I would pursue her heart, and hopefully, the rest would follow. I felt like this would be the hardest thing I would ever have to do, but thinking about her, I knew she was worth it. I'd never had to chase a chick, but I guess Miss Ava Boyd would be my first. Let the chase begin.

Six

M yah

It had been three weeks since our girls' trip and I already wanted to go back. I was in love with the Maldives to the point I asked my husband if we could retire there. I had been busy at the firm with my cousin working on her new branding campaign because there was a Human Resource aspect to it that would draw in a better candidate pool. It was only launched a week ago and we had already seen an increase in qualified applicants for various positions. I was proud of her and proud to work with her.

I had also been busy trying to staff our newest laundry mat in our chain. We took great pride in our laundry mats at Montgomery Wash & Fold and Montgomery Cleaners. The cleaners were a new addition to the chain, and they were located in the more affluent neighborhoods. We took a gamble on it two years ago and it definitely paid off. With competitive pricing and quick turnarounds, we came in and took over. Pushed a couple cleaners out of business, but hey, it was just business. All of our employees had benefits and I was very proud of that. I had worked a long day and was tired as hell, so I hope my husband didn't mind delivery tonight.

Driving up my driveway, I admired my house. We had it built from the ground up four years ago and it was everything I wanted. I didn't care if we were in this house forever. When I walked into my house and smelled food, I arched a brow. Anthony rarely cooked, but when he did, I prayed thanks to God. My husband could have been a chef I tell you. That's how his ass got my ass; he cooked one night for me after we had been dating for a while. I'm not ashamed to say I gave that man every corner of my honeypot that night and it's been a wrap ever since.

Putting my things down where they belonged, I walked to the kitchen to see a candlelight table set and it almost brought a tear to my eye. It had been a while since he'd done something like this. The smile that glowed on his handsome face reminded me why I fell in love.

"What I do to deserve this?" I inquired as I walked into his space to have him put his lips on me. His kiss was so deep that for a split second, I thought something was wrong. Don't get me wrong, my husband is affectionate, but this just felt different.

"You married me, that's what you did. You didn't turn your back on me, you helped me build and are still helping me build an empire. I love you for that and so much more." His stare was so intense, and my tear was a response to his words.

Wiping my tear and kissing me again, he pulled my chair out so I could sit. When he placed my plate in front of me with stuffed lobster linguine, I knew I was going to be bent up like a pretzel later. He could get it however he wanted it tonight because I already knew this was going to be the bomb.

We ate and talked about a little bit of everything and I just enjoyed talking to my husband, my best friend. This damn food was so good, I found myself dancing in my seat with him laughing at me. Anthony could cook his ass off, and I was happy tonight he decided to bless my taste buds.

"So, Myah, I wanted to talk to you about something." He shifted uncomfortably in his seat and I knew whatever it was had to be serious because he rarely called me Myah.

I cynically looked at him while placing my fork on my plate of Crème Brulee. "I swear, Anthony, if you cooked all this good food to tell me you're cheating on me or some crazy shit, I'm stabbing you with this fork, then eating your Crème Brulee as you bleed out."

His face tightened then released in a thunderous laugh. "Yo, I try to tell people you're crazy, but they don't believe me. What kinda woman stabs a man then eats his dessert?"

I didn't even say anything, but I turned my fork to a stabbing position. See, all I'm trying to do is live a life pleasing to the Lord and this man is about to have God temporarily mad at me. I've gone this long without having to commit a murder, that counts for something. Anthony trying to set me back.

"My, OK! I wanted to talk to you about having a baby."

Now that, I wasn't expecting. I was completely caught off guard. Putting my fork down, I rubbed my hands on my napkin and looked at my husband with concern.

"Anthony, I thought after what happened, you said you didn't want to have any babies by me?" The memory of what happened three years ago came rushing back and my emotional curtain was pulled back. I had worked so hard to close the curtain on this so it wouldn't affect me.

Anthony looked at me with squinted eyes. "My, I *never* said I didn't want babies by you. Are you serious? Is that what you've been carrying with you all these years, babe?"

That pissed me off, so I got up from my seat. "Anthony, if I remember correctly, after we lost AJ, you told me if I didn't get on birth control, you would leave me. You didn't want to have a baby."

Anthony dropped his head and I knew he knew that's exactly what he told me. "My, it wasn't that I didn't want you to have a baby again. I was scared. We lost AJ and I almost lost you, too. That shit terrified me, so I rather have just you and no children than a child without you. I know I was selfish because I know you want more kids. I just been thinking about it and I want that. I want that with you."

I couldn't hold it in anymore, the pain of it all. Three years ago, we were pregnant with our first son and I lost him at thirty-two weeks. I almost died as well from the loss of blood and trauma. It was a devastating loss and Anthony shut down the idea of ever having kids after that. That devasted me even more because, for as long as I have been able to think about it, I wanted a big family. I wanted to try again, but he was adamantly against it. We got into an argument and he told me if I didn't get on long term birth control, he would leave me. I left our home and went to my mother's house. Her and my father weren't together any longer because she decided one random day, she just didn't love him and left. It tore my father to shreds and caused issues in our relationship.

When I told her what he said, she told me, "You don't need a baby. You lost all that weight to be fat again. I was so happy when you lost the weight and thought you were crazy for getting pregnant in the first place."

My mother always had a way of tearing me down. I overheard her one time when I was younger, telling my father that I was fat because he let me do whatever and eat whatever I want. No man would ever want me because I was fat. I don't know, we had a weird relationship, but I let her thoughts get in my head, and the next day, I got on birth control. My husband and I never talked about kids again, so him saying this now caused a lot of emotions.

"I don't know, Anthony. Now I'm used to the thought of never having them. You did that. Let me think about it, please?" I asked and he nodded in agreement. This was a lot, and I really needed to think about it and talk to someone I could trust, but first, I would just think about it alone to make sure I was sound in mind before I spoke to anyone.

☙❧

IT HAD BEEN A MONTH SINCE ANTHONY ASKED ME TO HAVE a baby and I really thought it was like a one-off fluke, but I thought wrong. Every day, my loving husband had done things to make it clear that he wanted a baby. The first move was the next day after he asked. I woke up with a pair of baby shoes on my nightstand. The note said, "Our Baby's First Shoes."

Now a month later, I spent the day with Ava and came home to a damn playground in the corner of our backyard. This was like a super nice playground with all the setups of a park. How the hell did he do this in one damn Saturday? Ava thought it was the cutest thing and I wanted to chop his ass. She told me I was crazy to not have his baby and I had to look at her like she was a fool.

I was softening up, and I guess I had made my decision because I scheduled to have the birth control taken out of my arm tomorrow. All of the baby stuff made me want a baby and I realized he knew exactly what he was doing. Today, I was having a spa day with Ava, and it was time I get on her ass about Isaac. This man had been pursuing her with a passion and I felt bad for him. For the last month or so, he had literally sent her flowers or some type of gift every damn day. People at the firm just knew she had a new man. I told her she had better stop playing with that man before she misses out on something amazing.

"Girl, this sauna feels so good right now." Ava was laid out on the bench above me. We had been in here for only about ten minutes, but I personally was ready to get out. The sauna was her thing, but I wanted to talk to her since this spa had private saunas.

"I bet it do. Look, girl, when you gon' stop playing with Isaac's fine ass? He been coming at you hard as hell." I didn't feel like postponing this talk.

With an aggravated huff, she tried to be a smart ass. "I'll give Isaac the time of day when you agree to give Anthony a baby. How about that, bitch?"

Oh, she's really mad because rarely, and I do mean rarely, do we address each other as bitches. It just wasn't something we did. I had something for that ass, though.

"Well, I guess you're going to be giving him the time of day after tomorrow since I get my birth control out then... bitch." With a smirk, I got up and walked out of the sauna. Ava was on my heels.

"Wait, what? You...you are really going to give Anthony a baby? I'm going to be an auntie?" Her smile was so big, it made me smile. Ava would make an amazing mother if she just allowed herself to love again.

"Yes, I'm going to give that big head man a high yellow baby. I'm not going to tell him I'm taking it out, though. I'm just going to let God do His thing." I smiled at the thought of him finding out I was pregnant. I know he said this was what he wanted; I prayed it really was.

Seven

A^{va}

Busy was not even a proper word to describe how busy it had been since I'd been back from vacation. My team hit the ground running on our branding campaign and we were already getting a return on our work. I was so proud of my team and also my cousin. Myah had been by my side the entire way. My campaign had a recruiting aspect to it for developing a more qualified candidate pool that she assisted me with. Her team was working just as heavily. I loved my career and my firm. We had unmatched benefits and a retirement plan, we also had a pension plan, which was something you didn't see a lot of these days.

Isaac, that man is just relentless. For almost two months, he had sent me gifts of some kind. When I say gifts, I'm not talking about some Harris Teeter roses. I'd gotten four dozen La Fleur Bouquet Roses. I don't know if he just knew I loved only pink, blue, and white roses, but that's what I got, never red. I was in awe of his effort in wanting to talk to me. He called me, which I had no idea how he got my office, home, and cell number, but that's a story for another day. We had been talking on the phone, but I didn't tell Myah because I didn't want to give her false hope. I just really liked talking to him and his sexy ass voice had brought me to many orgasms, unbeknownst to him.

Today, he casually told me he was having lunch at Aria at twelve-thirty and I love Aria, so I decided to stop in. There's nothing wrong with just conversation, right? I haven't said anything to lead him on and I told him to stop with the gifts, but he refuses. God, the man is everything! He does things that my husband didn't even do, and I feel bad in that. I missed Andre so much 'til it hurt sometimes. God has a cruel sense of humor.

Walking into Aria, I looked around for Isaac but didn't see him. The hostess approached me with a wide smile, so I smiled back.

"Hi, Ava. How are you?" she asked in the most pleasant voice like I wasn't about to sidestep her on how she knew my name. My face clearly showed my confusion. "Isaac is waiting for you, right this way."

Does this man think of everything? I didn't even confirm I was coming. It amazes me because Isaac has this street edge to him to the point you would think he would not be this romantic or sentimental, but in conversation, I learned he comes from a two-parent household that was filled with love. He explained the love of his parents, so I understood the cloth he was cut from. Walking into the room, Isaac stood to receive me, and I almost wanted to walk out because the devil was busy. Why does this man have on gray sweats? One thing about me, as corporate as I am, I don't like corporate men. My husband was much like Isaac. We met freshman year of college and started dating about four months into the year. We had been together ever since and married during graduate school in 2009. God, I miss him so much.

"Hey, beautiful, how are you?" I walked into his awaiting arms and it felt good. Our height difference was perfect, and his natural scent was just amazing.

Pulling away and looking up into his handsome face, I smiled at his smile. "Hey, handsome. How did you know I was coming?"

He gave me a chuckle before he answered. "I had a hunch."

We sat, ate, and just talked. He is an amazing person and any woman would be blessed to have him on their arm. He definitely is sexy as hell. I wanted to give him a chance, and now that Myah had taken the birth control out almost three months ago, I said that I would agree to a date if he asked. Luckily, he had yet to ask. A part of me wanted him to, but another part was scared that he would. I just didn't know if love was for me anymore. My heart was still raw from the events of the past. Could I love? Was I worthy of love?

"Hey, I lost you for a minute. Where'd you go?" His deep voice brought me out of my daze.

"I'm sorry, my mind wanders from time to time. Just thinking." I gave him his attention back.

"Damn, if you drifting off while I'm in your presence, then I need to get up on my job."

I dropped my head in laughter.

Reaching my hand out to him, we connected. I felt the spark that I was afraid of causing me to pull back. "I won't do it again, bae...I mean Isaac, Isaac."

The smirk he gave me let me know my slip of the tongue was not missed. Uuggh! It did feel natural coming off of my tongue, but it was a mistake. He didn't even let the slip get up before addressing it.

"Well, since I'm Bae and all... Bae wants to take you on a

date." And there it was! Damn, the Bae! I told Myah if he asked, I would say yes, and I was a woman of my word.

With a roll of my eyes, I questioned, "When does Bae want to take me out?"

"I want all of your Saturday." My eyes bugged out to his response.

"All of my Saturday? Isaac, what kind of date takes all day?" I was curious now. I had never been on an all-day date.

Isaac placed both of his elbows on the table and it was as if he was staring into my soul. "Ava, let me explain something to you very early and you can make the determination if you want to deal with it. I'm a selfish man and when I have you, you belong to me. Right now, you belong to me. Soon, hopefully, you will be mine whether you are in my presence or not. I want to show you early on what life will be like with me."

Now that was deep and sexy as fuck! *God, why are You doing this to me?*

"OK, well Saturday is fine. I will clear my calendar. What time should I expect you?"

He pressed some buttons on his phone and looked off as if he was trying to decide. "Let's say eight-thirty. Shoot me your email and I'll have a car pick you up. I'll text you everything that you will need."

Everything I need? This is definitely going to be interesting, and I honestly was looking forward to it. I might as well go with the flow and see what happens because there is never anything wrong with being with a fine ass man for a whole day.

It was Friday night and I spent the latter part of the day getting my hair, nails, and feet done. Isaac's text came through around seven-thirty and I called Myah to come over and have some wine with me.

"Girl, read me the text but you gotta read it in his voice." Myah knew her request was silly based on her outburst of laughter. Just as silly as the request was, I was sillier because I was going to do it.

"Baby Girl! You don't know how happy I am that you finally letting a nigga take you out for real. Saturday is officially the first of what I hope are many "Ava's Days". For Ava's Day, I need you to wear something comfortable (I.e. legging, sneakers, etc.). Your hair might get wet, hope you don't mind. I'll pay for it to get redone. We are going to breakfast first, of course, then I have an adventure planned. After our adventure, bring a change of comfortable clothes (jeans, sandals, etc.). We are going to continue our date with lunch and a couples massage. You will need another change of clothes, something dressy because we are going on a dinner cruise. I pray everything that I have planned is to your liking. Can't wait to see you in the morning."

I laughed at myself trying to imitate Isaac's deep-set voice.

Myah and I were falling over with the humor of the moment. I love being with Myah because she always kept a smile on my face. She had been my best friend since we were basically in diapers. She had been with me through everything that I had endured, and I knew she would always be with me.

"Girl, that man pulling out all of the stops for this first date. I swear you better not hold yourself back from having fun with this man. Ava, you deserve this, baby. It's time for you to love again. You have to have faith that God has sent someone to love you and help you on your road to wholeness." Her words brought tears to my eyes, or maybe the wine did. Nonetheless, I was crying now.

Tomorrow would be a great day, and I would make sure that I let myself enjoy him and me being with him. This would be a new thing for me. I had never been with any other man except Andre. He was my first in everything. I feel guilty about moving on from him. Will he think I didn't love him? I was scared but I promised Myah I would try.

⚜

THE NEXT MORNING, I WAS UP EARLY, READY FOR MY DAY. I was so excited that I was literally dancing around the house. I decided to wear a bathing suit under a Victoria's Secret Pink leggings set. I had a bag packed with the outfits that were requested that Myah helped me pick. Looking in the mirror, I smiled at how cute I was today. I decided to not wear makeup since we may get wet. Hearing my doorbell, I looked at my clock on the wall and it was eight-thirty on the dot. Grabbing my bag, I headed to the door, and when I answered, I was pleasantly pleased. This man is fine!

I swear him wearing sweatpants out in public should be a crime. I could say this in a pretty, ladylike way, but at the end of the day, this nigga had a big ass dick. He had his locs in a fishtail braid and some aviator shades on. *Damn, God, why are You doing me like this?*

"Hey, Baby Girl, you look good as fuck." He pulled me in his arms, and I melted from his touch.

"Hey, I'm ready." He nodded his head and grabbed my bag. I thought he was driving but we had a driver. Sliding in the back seat, he sat close to me and I definitely didn't mind. Well, let the day begin.

Eight

I saac

THE TIME HAD FINALLY COME! AFTER ALMOST TWO MONTHS of trying to make Ava see that I wanted her, she finally gave in. She didn't know because I swore her to secrecy, but Myah had been helping me along the way. Telling me her favorite things, she helped me plan the date that we were going on. I planned this date a month in advance. I always knew I planned to ask her to go out with me on this day when I came up with the thought of Ava's Day. I wanted her to feel special and know that she was worth every ounce of my time, uninterrupted. This was a no-phone date. When I told her I wanted us to leave our phones in the car, she had a little attitude, but she got over it really quickly.

Sitting next to her on our way to breakfast, I loved just being able to be so close to her.

We ate breakfast at her favorite place, Terrace Café, then we were on our way to Carowinds. I had previously asked her if she liked amusement parks and she said she loved them, so that would be our first part of the day. When we made it inside, we had our picture taken, and I told her I wanted to buy it before we left because this would be our memory of where it began. We were all over that damn park and I loved seeing her laugh and be carefree. She was most beautiful when she was carefree. Ava went crazy when we made it to the waterpark, and I loved every damn second of it.

"Girl, come here!" I yelled as Ava ran from me, but it didn't take long for me to catch her and toss her over my shoulder. She had on this cute ass two-piece bikini and the way her ass shook as she ran was something I never wanted to forget.

"Isaac, wait! I won't do it again!" She was screaming louder than the kids in the area and I couldn't stop laughing. I ran in the wave pool and we both got caught in the wave, but I held her tight. We came from under the water in laughter. Looking into her eyes, I took my shot and kissed her lips. She kissed me back, but when I tried again, she pulled away and I felt the wall coming back up.

Ava tried to move from my arms, but I pulled her back to me. "Ava, baby, don't do that. We were doing good, let's not go back to that place."

Her eyes saddened, but she didn't move from my hold. I kissed her lips again and she let me. Her lips were so soft. I didn't want to push it, so I left it at that. We got done at the park around one-thirty in the afternoon, so we cleaned ourselves up and headed to lunch. Myah told me Ava loved Fatz Café but rarely went, so I made sure we went there for lunch. One thing I loved about Ava was her ass was not cute when it comes to eating. Her ass ate like six of their lemon poppyseed rolls.

"You want some more rolls, bae?" I asked her with an arched brow.

She looked at me with a smirk.

"Hush! Stop making fun of me. I like to eat."

I laughed at her pout. When our food came, we ate and talked as we always did about a little bit of everything. Once we finished eating, we left, but not without getting some rolls to go.

Our next portion of her day was the couples massage and a nigga had to keep his dick at bay because she undressed in front of me. Yes, I'd seen her in a bathing suit and all that, but the way she undressed was sexy as fuck. As if she was doing it just for my benefit, and believe me, I didn't mind.

"So, what you think about your day so far?" I asked as we were getting massaged.

She opened her eyes and looked at me and I could swear they were watery. "No one has ever made me feel this special, not even my husband. You didn't have to do all of this. A simple movie and dinner would have sufficed."

I shook my head at her thinking she was not worthy of this level of care. My dad took care of my mom on this level, if not better, and he always told me this was how you take care of who you love among other things. We care for the things we cherish.

"Movies and dinner are not a date with me and you. That's just something to do, Ava. Don't worry, you'll get used to this level of care. Anything less is uncivilized."

By the time we were finished with our massage, it was going on four-thirty and the dinner cruise left at seven-forty-five. I got us a hotel room so we could just relax, shower and change. I made sure it was a suite with a living area so she would feel comfortable and not think I had expectations of sex. Now if she offered, I was going to murder that cat and claim it as my own, but nah, that wasn't my intention. I could tell she was nervous when we got to the hotel, but I explained it and she loosened up.

Once we got in the room, she showered immediately and got comfortable. Even in the simplest of clothing, she was amazingly beautiful, and I was happy to get to experience her in this light. Time seemed to fly to the point we almost didn't want to go on the cruise, but I knew her ass was going to be hungry again. We separated to get dressed for the night and when she came out of the room with her dress on, I had to step back and take her in. Damn.

"If ever heaven sent an angel, it would look like you," I told her as I walked to her and placed a kiss on her lips. She was still giving me resistance on kissing, but she accepted pecks. I was going to break her out of that shit. Those were going to be my lips. I could smell the Gucci Guilty on her and it complemented her natural scent well.

"You look so handsome. Don't have me out here fighting these females over your fine ass, Isaac." I drew back and feigned shock.

"Me? I would never. I'm just a black ass boy trying to make it, don't anyone want me."

We shared a laugh and were on our way.

◌⁕◌

THE DINNER CRUISE WAS NICE AS HELL. THERE WAS A cocktail hour as soon as we got on the boat and we drank and ate on appetizers as we listened to a live jazz band. My babe could dance, and I was amused and pleased at the same time to have her in my arms as we swayed to the music on the floor. Her hips kept the rhythm and my hands had a mind of their own when they cuffed her ass. I could tell it surprised her because her body stiffened a little, but then relaxed as we danced. That ass was soft, so I was happy she didn't make me move my hands.

"You two make such a lovely couple." Our dancing moment was interrupted by the comment of an older couple dancing next to us.

"Thank you, ma'am. I'm trying to make this little lady my one if she allows me to. She's putting up a good fight, though, been denying me for almost three months," I said as I looked at Ava and gave her a wink and a smile. My favorite thing happened after that, her skin tone took on that rosy, reddish blushing color. I made a mental note to find something that color for her to explain how that makes me feel.

When dinner was served, we enjoyed a nice salad with this vinaigrette dressing that my babe really liked, and I made a note to ask the chef what it was so I could get her some for home. I was that man. If my babe wanted it, I was going to make it happen. The main course was a rack of lamb and steak. She had the lamb; I had the steak. Technically, she had both because this girl ate off of my damn plate, too. All I could do was laugh at her and let her have her way like I knew I damn near always would. We happened to sit next to the couple from earlier, so we enjoyed conversation between us. We learned a lot about the couple, and it was a blessing to see a couple that had been married for fifty-seven years. While we were talking, there was a point I could tell Ava was thinking about her late husband, so I placed my hand on her leg to bring her back to me.

"Come back to me, babe."

She looked at me and gave me a weak smile.

It was never my intention to replace her late husband or even try to make her forget him. I just wanted to carry on the torch of loving her the way she deserved and needed to be loved. It was really as simple as that. I wanted her to feel comfort in that and not feel guilty for moving on. I knew she would always love him, and I was not trying to take over that portion of her heart. He rightfully earned that and could have it, but the rest would belong to me, and hopefully our future children. We ate Crème Brulee for dessert; well, she did because I had a spoonful and she had the rest. I swear her little ass could eat and I loved that shit.

After dinner, the cruise got live as hell with a DJ and Ava could damn dance. The way her ass tooted up on my dick was going to be a damn problem if she didn't keep her little thick ass still in this dress. Grabbing her around her waist, I put my lips to her ear to speak.

"Aye, you better keep still before I have to introduce you to the beast when we get back to the room." I kissed her neck behind her ear, and I felt her body stiffen.

She moved away from me and I couldn't really read the look in her eyes. She told me she had to use the restroom, so I let her go. Damn, I hope I didn't speak out of turn because pulling Ava's walls down was like a full-time job. I was tired of the shit if I was being honest, and tonight would really determine if I was going to continue to pursue her. Yes, I wanted her, but I was not going to allow my heart to be played with. Yea, I may be reformed, but I'm a street nigga to the heart and this was just not how we handle females to some extent. I was blessed to be in a loving household, and I had no business actually being in the streets. A hard head definitely made a soft behind when I had to be sent up the road for four years, but I was cool because I was with my nigga Anthony.

Ava stayed in the damn bathroom or wherever she was until we docked and was ready to get off the boat. I can't even lie and say I wasn't mad because I was. I chose to wait until we got back to the room to address it. When we walked in, I saw her on her phone so I walked over to look and she was ordering an Uber.

"Yo, did I do or say something wrong, lil' mama? Let me know what it really is," I frustratingly questioned her.

When she gave me her eyes, they were glossed over.

"Isaac, I like you, but I just can't. We shouldn't talk anymore."

That blew me, and although I didn't want to, I needed her to see my frustration mixed with a little bit of anger.

"Ava, real talk, though, you're gonna have to tell a nigga something. I don't get this shit. Why are you blocking this? You don't think I'm good enough for your corporate ass or some shit?" I was standing in front of her with my arms across my chest.

She moved away from me before speaking. "Isaac, don't be ridiculous. It's not you that is not good enough, I'm not good enough for you. I just think it's best we not talk."

I still wasn't understanding that shit at all and I needed more. I felt like I deserved it. This was a weird space for me because again, I don't sweat females.

"Nah, ma. You gonna have to give me more than that lame ass shit. Are you fucking with someone else you like better? Are you still in love with your husband? What, Ava?"

At the mention of her late husband, her facial expression changed and I could tell I struck a nerve. She let out a loud chuckle.

"This is the cruelest punishment God could have given me. If losing my husband wasn't enough and everything else, He put me here. I swear." I was lost to that statement.

"What the fuck are you talking about?" I was so over this shit and just wanted clarity.

Ava stood to her feet across the room where she was and crossed her arms over her chest in a defiant stance.

"You want to know why I'm pulling back? Why I don't think I deserve you? Why you should just move the fuck on, Isaac? You want to hear the fucking words?"

This is the first I've heard her curse and it was sexy, but I had to stay focused. "Fuck yeah, I wouldn't be fucking asking if I didn't, little ass girl."

With a chuckle, she gave me an answer I was not prepared for. "OK, Isaac. Here is it. I'm HIV positive. Still want me now?"

Nine

A va

YEAH, I'M HIV POSITIVE. IT WASN'T SOMETHING I WANTED for my life, and if I could change it, I definitely would. I never saw this for my life, but it happened. That's why I tried to keep to myself. I don't date for a reason. Who wants to have this conversation with people? If I don't date, I can't fall for anyone and no one can fall for me. It's really that simple. Now, look. Isaac is literally stuck, as if he's trying to process the words that just came out of my mouth.

"Wait, what did you just say?" The look on his face was unreadable.

Speaking in a slower pace, I restated my comment. "I am HIV positive, and so we are clear before you freak out, you can't get it from kissing me or touching me. You're safe."

He took a step back from me and there was a look of disbelief, which I expected. I could tell he had questions and I wondered how this would end. I made sure I stayed near the door, just in case I needed to make a quick escape. I'm not foolish in this situation, and if it turned violent, I wanted to be ready.

"What do you mean you're HIV positive? You...you don't look sick, Ava. How is that even possible? So, you were like a hoe or some shit?" He looked so confused and his question hurt. Why is it that every person that becomes HIV positive has to have been a hoe, gay, or a drug user, as if that is a reason to deserve this?

All I could do was chuckle through the hurt of the question. "No, I was not a hoe. If you must know, I have never been with anyone except my husband. I contracted it from him."

His eyes almost fell out of his head. He started pacing and that made me nervous. I moved closer to the door. Isaac stopped pacing and looked at me with daggers in his eyes.

"Why are you scooting towards the door? You think I'm going to hurt you or some shit? I'm not built like that, little mama, regardless of this fucked up situation, so you can chill." He said it as if I offended him.

Feeling my phone vibrate, I looked to see that my Uber had arrived. I felt like it was God telling me to get the hell out of here. I was so happy that when I first came in the room, I moved my bag to the chair near the door.

"Hey, my Uber is here. Thank you for tonight. You made me feel very special and I appreciate you for that. I know this is probably the last time I'll talk to you, and that's cool, I really did like you, but I definitely understand you not wanting to deal with me."

Picking up my bag and opening the room door, I looked at him and he still looked confused. I fought my tears and said goodbye to someone that I could have had a future with. God was being cruel and I didn't understand what I had done to ever deserve this. I was a good and faithful girlfriend and wife. *Why me, God?*

Ten

I saac

WHAT THE FUCK JUST HAPPENED? I WAS REPLAYING THE whole fucking night in my head and was coming up blank. Ava just told me she is HIV positive. Like, you got to be kidding me. There is no way that girl is HIV positive. Damn, she doesn't look sick at all, and she fine as fuck. How could she have something like HIV? Then she said she got that shit from her damn husband! Like, that's why that nigga died? That's some crazy shit, and I was in shock, still standing in the same spot since she walked out of this hotel room about ten minutes ago.

Wait, she's Myah's cousin, so that means Myah probably knows that shit. Myah tells Anthony ass every-fucking-thing so this nigga was going to let me hook up with Ava, knowing she had the damn ninja. Yeah, I was going to throw hands with my boy when I saw him in the damn morning. We had a Sunday ritual, especially during football season. Myah always does brunch with Ava on Sunday, and while they were out, we got up together to play Madden or whatever game was popping, drink, ate and talk. That was our version of brunch. Yeah, he was going to have to tell me something because this right here was a no fucking go. I couldn't believe that damn girl had the ninja.

Looking around the room, I thought about the fact that I wanted to have sex with her. I mean, I didn't expect it, but I did want to. Crazy! I know one thing; I definitely wasn't going to waste this room so I was going to sleep here tonight like I planned. Well, actually, I never planned to be alone. No wonder her ass was pushing me off. I should have let her ass, but no, I had to have her. Damn.

৩ৡৣ৩

THE NEXT MORNING, I GOT UP AROUND NINE AND showered so I could leave and head to Anthony's house in Ballantyne. I had parked my personal car in the hotel parking lot yesterday before I got the day started so I would be able to drive this morning. As I drove to Anthony's house, I was still in shock. Damn, Ava has HIV. How the fuck does someone as beautiful as her have something like that? She was sexy as fuck and a damn executive at her firm. For all intents and purposes, she's a boss. Pulling up to Andre and Myah's house, I knew that she was already gone. Walking to the door, I placed my fingerprint on the scanner. This dude was fancy and had this security firm Lourie's Security set up the security in their home, which included keyless entry. When I stepped in the house, it announced that it was me. I knew he was in his mancave, so I headed straight there.

When I walked in the room, he was sitting on his couch, smoking his morning blunt. He looked at me with this damn smirk on his face and I got mad all over again.

"What's up, bro? How was your Ava's Day?" He chuckled.

I wanted to punch that man in his damn face. "Man, fuck you. How the hell you just not going to tell me that damn girl is sick?"

He looked at me confused as hell. "What the hell you talking about?" He took a pull from the blunt.

"Nigga, that girl is HIV positive."

Anthony choked on the smoke he had just taken in. He was coughing hard as hell, so I got up and got him a water out of the fridge in the mancave. He drank the whole damn bottle before he started talking.

"Bruh, what the hell you talking about? I didn't know that."

I looked at him with a side eye. Now I know as close as Myah and Ava are that she knows, so I found it hard to believe she didn't tell her husband.

"Come on, man. You can't make me believe Myah doesn't know and she tells your ass everything." I just couldn't believe this dude didn't know.

He looked at me with the most serious look. "Isaac, I put it on everything I love, I didn't know. My wife never told me no shit like that. You think I would let you talk to someone who has damn AIDS? Man, I wouldn't do you like that.

"Maybe Myah doesn't know. I can't see my wife holding something like this from me. Nah, not my, and if she did, we have a damn problem. Ava done been all up and through my house. Cooking, cleaning, showering and using my damn bathrooms. How the hell did she get that shit, man?" Anthony was shaking his head and I knew just like me, he was trying to put it all together.

"She said she wasn't a hoe or nothing. She had only been with her husband. He gave her that shit, man. You think that's why he died?" I wondered if he knew why he died because it was just crazy.

"Man, I don't even really know. I mean, dude was cool, but

we weren't tight. We went out on a couple of double dates at the girls' insistence, but you know I don't really do new friends. All I know is his ass went to the hospital with pneumonia and never came out. That's what the hell Myah's ass told me." Anthony was out of his seat going to his bar.

"Aye, pour me one, too, man." I needed a drink like I needed air right now.

He brought me my drink and sat down. I think we sat on his couch for ten minutes before either of us spoke again.

Anthony broke the silence. "So, what you gonna do?"

I looked at him with a crooked neck like he was crazy. "What you mean, what am I going to do? I'm not messing with that girl. Hell no, won't have me dying slowly. Shit is a shame too because I really, really, really like Ma. Damn, what are the odds?"

We sat there before I asked him what was up with him and Myah making a baby.

"Man, I don't even know. She ain't really said anything about it," he said in frustration.

"Well, is she still on birth control?"

"I really don't even know. I do know I've been letting loose in her every chance I get. Your mom and pops made me realize how selfish I was when we lost AJ. I don't want to do that to My. I love the ground that thick ass girl walks on and having a little me or her walking around here would be the icing on the cake. Dog, could you imagine a little Myah running around here?" His smile was wide as he spoke.

I remember when they were pregnant with AJ, Anthony was the proudest I had ever seen him. He loved his wife with a vengeance and that was something I always admired about him. Girls stay on his light skinned, light eyes ass but he curved bitches so hard. I remember back in the day, this fool used to carry around those little ass pictures you used to get in a photo packet that no one used. The ones that were smaller than a wallet size. Well, he used to carry around like twenty of them at a damn time. Anytime we went out and a chick pushed up on him, he would give her ass the picture of Myah and be like when you see her, know that I'm all hers. I thought it was the corniest thing I had ever seen, but what was funny was females used to get mad hot over it.

"Man, if you have a little Myah running around here, we both might have to get more guns or something. We're gonna have issues from the sandbox."

We both gave off a loud laugh. I will never deny Myah is gorgeous as hell and thick with it. We both loved thick women. Ava was slimmer thick, but thick, nonetheless. Uuggh! Why am I still thinking about her?

Anthony looked like he was in thought.

"Man, now some stuff is starting to make sense. I remember like a year after Ava's husband died, she went through this deep ass depression and even tried to kill herself. I always just linked it to her missing her husband, but if she has that package, it may have been more than just her missing him. Damn, that's messed up that he gave her that thing. Cheating ain't worth it, man. I stay loyal to my wife, to hell with all that other stuff."

It seemed like she was a good girl that just got with the wrong dude. I was still thrown off because the way she referenced her husband, it was like she still loved him. I don't know if I could still love someone who sentenced me to death. I don't know if I could do that at all.

I chilled with Anthony for a little while longer and we got a game in, but then I left to go home. I lived in the South-Park area in a townhome that I owned. I felt like I was still in a bad dream or something and maybe I could sleep it off.

Getting in my house, I threw my bag on the couch and it fell off from the force in which I threw it. I walked over to pick it up, and when I did, left on the floor was the little keychain I got from Carowinds with Ava and my picture in it. I looked in the little hole at the picture and shook my head. I was standing behind her with my arms wrapped around her and she was smiling big. I can't believe her ass has AIDS. Out of all the females I take a serious liking to, I pick the one who is sick. I had spent damn near two months talking to her on the phone and getting to know her; why wouldn't she just tell me this from jump, so I didn't waste my time? I was tired and needed to sleep this off; maybe when I wake up, it would all have been a bad ass dream.

CHAPTER 11

A nthony Montgomery

I HAD BEEN PUTTING IN OVERTIME WITH MYAH BECAUSE I wanted a baby. I knew I flipped out on her when we lost AJ, but I was scared as hell when I almost lost her, too. Myah is my everything. Meeting her was the best thing that could have happened to me and I thank God every day for letting her see past my rough exterior to my good heart. I was a straight knucklehead when I was younger and got in a lot of trouble. My parents were too busy partying and doing their own thing, but when the Mills moved here, everything changed.

I met Isaac when some dudes were trying to jump him, and I just didn't think that was right, especially knowing he was new to the neighborhood. I jumped in and we whooped ass. We'd been thick as thieves ever since. His mom and dad took me under their wing, and I love them like my own mom and dad. As for my mom and dad, they died together when I was eighteen and they tried to rob someone. It was an unfortunate situation and event, but I will not lie and say I was torn up about it. If I saw my parents once a week, that was a treat. I had basically moved in with the Mills by the time I was fifteen, and Pop Mills had been cutting my hair ever since.

After I went up the road and came home, I tried to get a job, but just having a high school diploma and a criminal record proved to be a disadvantage in every sense of the word. I met Myah when I applied for a warehouse job and she was the recruiting coordinator. We got to know each other a tiny bit since she was my direct point of contact, but I didn't get the job. When I saw her some time later out in the streets, I took my shot and it was a slam dunk. Myah changed my fucking life. She convinced me to use the money I had stashed to start a business. That's when I met Ava; she helped her with the business plan and marketing plan.

I love Myah and knew from that day she was going to be my wife and I made it happen. We were best friends, so to think that she kept something this serious a secret from me was blowing me. We told each other everything, to my knowledge. She knows my most embarrassing secrets to my most gruesome ones. Isaac dropping that bomb on me had me feeling a way because I remember the time when Ava lost her husband. That was the toughest part of our marriage because I felt like she was doing too much. When she got pregnant, I was on her ass, but she still was running behind Ava and I just didn't understand. Now with this new knowledge, it made complete sense. With the stress of all of that, I wonder if it had anything to do with Myah losing my son.

Hearing the alarm go off, letting me know Myah had

entered the house, I looked at the clock, seeing it was after two in the afternoon. I didn't move from my space in my mancave because I knew she would come in here. It took her about ten minutes before she came in and sat down.

"Hey, babe." She sat next to me and kissed my lips. I looked at her and just shook my head.

"Myah, is there something you need to tell me?" I returned my gaze to her.

"Not really, did you have a good morning with Isaac?" Oh, she's playing games I see. Let me stop playing with her beautiful ass before I get caught up.

"Myah, don't fucking play with me. Isaac already told me." Myah shrugged her shoulder to my statement and got her ass up.

"Well, if you know, ain't nothing to tell you, right? What you want to do for dinner?" This damn girl walked out my mancave like it was cool and I was on her tail.

"Myah, you got me fucked up. How did you feel it was OK to not tell me that damn girl is HIV positive and I was hooking my best friend up with her? You know how flaw that makes me look?" She spun around so fast, she almost damn near fell.

"Anthony, are you serious right now? What difference does it make if I told you? She's the same fucking Ava. She told me when we first found out to tell you, but I chose not to because I didn't want you looking at her differently. Plus, how are you flawed for hooking your best friend up with an amazing woman?" Her skin was turning red and I knew she was fire mad, but I didn't care.

I laughed at her ass. "An awesome woman with a fucking package; you must be out yo' rabbit ass mind. Plus, she's been all up and through our house like it's hers. Man, let me go to Sam's Club and buy some disinfectant and clean my fucking house."

The hard-handed slap across my face was not expected because we never got physical with each other, so for her to put her hands on me was serious. The tears that came from her eyes let me know that I had hurt her.

"I never realized I married an ignorant son of a bitch until this moment. You can't get HIV from touching things, stupid. While you take your stupid ass down to Sam's to get that shit, I'll be at my cousin's house." She turned and walked down the hall.

Before she reached the end of the hall, she stopped and dug in her purse that was still on her shoulder. When she turned around to face me, her face was drenched in tears. She lifted her arms and threw something at me.

"Congratulations, bitch." My eye twitched at her calling me a bitch because that, too, was something we didn't do. We didn't talk to each other like this. I kept my eyes on the hallway until I heard the alarm alert that the door had opened and closed.

Looking down on the floor at what she threw at me, my heart tried to jump out of my chest. My babe is pregnant. I didn't even know she had taken the damn birth control out, and now she was mad and pregnant. Fuck!

🦋

"DOG, MYAH GOT ME FUCKED UP. HER ASS BLOCKED ME ON all her social media, email and her phone. I haven't seen or heard from My for four damn days." I was mad as hell that my pregnant wife was playing with me. I wanted her ass here with me so I could rub on her belly. I didn't know anything about the pregnancy right now and that had my anxiety on high.

"I'm sure she's OK. She's probably with Ava, have you called her?" I didn't even think of calling her, but I felt awkward. I was going to have to get over that feeling because I wanted my wife. Pulling out my phone, I found Ava's number in my contacts and called the number, placing it on speaker.

"Hello," Ava answered on the third ring.

"Uuum... Hey, Ava, it's Anthony. How are you?" I was actually nervous talking to her.

"Hi, Anthony. I've been better, you know, having HIV and all, but hey...you already know that." Damn, I looked at Isaac and he had his head lowered.

"Yeah, about that. Sorry to hear that." I was sympathetic to it. It was crazy.

"Oh, no worries. I hope you got the disinfectant I sent to you. Make sure you get every nook and cranny. I wouldn't want you to die or anything, you know, since I'm the walking dead. Anyway, you call for your pregnant, getting on my nerves, throwing up all day wife?" Ava was holding nothing back and I looked at Isaac, who shook his head at me.

Two days ago, this damn girl sent me fifty canisters of Clorox wipes from Amazon with a note that said, "For your cleaning pleasure, asshole." I felt bad as hell because I loved Ava like my little sister. This shouldn't have changed how I looked or felt about her. There was so much I just didn't know about the disease.

"Uuum, yeah. Can I talk to her?" I didn't even want to address her about the other stuff. Ava and Myah were twins when it came to having an assassin tongue. I'd never met two women that could kill you kindly with words.

"I shouldn't let you, but after spending all damn night in the hospital with her, she needs to talk to you." I jumped out of my seat at the mention of My being at the hospital.

"Hospital! Why didn't she call me? Is she OK? Is my baby OK?" I had my keys in my hand and was heading to the door with Isaac on my heels.

"That was her decision. Even though you're an asshole, I told her to call you," Ava said before I heard ruffling on the phone. I heard her telling Myah I was on the phone and she said she didn't want to talk to me. I was on my way to her, so she was going to see me. After a couple words more, my wife finally got on the phone.

"Yes, Anthony?" The way she said my name pissed me off, but I kept my attitude at a minimum.

"My, babe. Why didn't you call me when you went to the hospital? Babe, I need you to come home so I can take care of you and my baby." I heard her sniffle. My heart was hurting because I was a man that couldn't take my wife crying.

"Anthony, I just can't right now. I'm fine here with my sick cousin. It hurt finding out your love is conditional." I looked over at Isaac, who had a solemn look on his face.

"Ight, My." I hung the phone up.

She had me fucked up if she thought I wasn't coming for her. My love was nowhere near conditional, I was just shocked. I didn't know what I didn't know. Sure, the disinfectant comment was an asshole move and I could admit that as a man. I loved Ava and I feel fucked up about her having to live with this, but damn. I'm not about to lose my wife over this, hell no.

It took me about twenty minutes to get to Ava's condo building and park in the underground garage. I had a pass to her building, so it was no issue getting in. Ava had a fly ass penthouse condo on the twenty-first floor of a high rise in uptown Charlotte. She had a dope ass view of the Bank of America stadium. Getting off the elevator, there were only two apartments on this floor. I knocked on the door and looked at Isaac. My dude looked nervous as hell. When Ava answered the door, I looked at Isaac again and I saw it all on his face. He loved this damn girl.

"Where is she?" I asked Ava as she moved to the side and let us in.

"She's in the guest bathroom, throwing up." I didn't wait to hear anything else. I headed to my wife.

Twelve

Four Days ago, Late Afternoon...
Myah

I WAS PISSED OFF FOR A NUMBER OF REASON, BUT THE MAIN one was why wouldn't Ava tell me that she told Isaac about her status? We sat at brunch for hours and she glowed about her damn Ava's Day and how much she liked Isaac but neglected to tell me she told him her status. I was completely blindsided by Anthony and I didn't appreciate that at all. I found out I was pregnant Saturday afternoon and she was the first person I told at brunch. We were both so excited about it and I couldn't wait to get home to tell Anthony, but then he hit me with this shit.

Now I had a mad ass husband and a baby in my belly. Driving to Ava's condo, I was trying to understand it all. She could have told me so I was prepared when I walked into my house. She knew I didn't tell Anthony even though she told me I could. I didn't want to because, frankly, it was none of his business. We weren't at risk of "catching" it, so what was the point of having him look at my cousin differently? She didn't ask for this. It didn't take me long to get to Ava's condo, and when I did, I came in ready to beat her ass.

"AVA! WHERE ARE YOU?" I came in yelling even though I saw her ass sitting on the couch. She looked at me from the couch with an arched brow.

"Girl, what is wrong with you?" She looked at me in confusion.

"So, you didn't think it was a need to know that you told damn Isaac about your damn status? Did you not think he would tell Anthony? I just walked into a damn ambush and you left me out to damn hang. How could you?" I had my hands on my hips while she was sitting on the couch, looking at me. When her eyes watered, my resolve broke and I softened.

"Myah, I was embarrassed. I told you I didn't want to do this, and look what happened. He looked at me like I was the scum of the earth. I really liked him, Myah." Her tears fell freely and I moved to her, pulling her into my arms.

I never thought about that. I never thought about the embarrassment that would come from the rejection. How could I not think of that? I just sat with her and let her cry. No words were needed because her tears told her story. Of course, my pregnant, emotional ass cried with her. After we both calmed down, I told her about Anthony's ignorant ass and that I was staying with her until further notice. I knew it wouldn't last long, especially after I blocked all communication from him after the second day.

Present Day...

I was sick as a damn dog. I didn't remember being this sick with AJ. I threw up so much over the last two days, I had to go to the hospital last night and get fluids. I was exhausted from throwing up and I just wanted it to stop. They gave me some pills to help, but I hated taking pills; hell, I was planning to take vitamin gummies. I couldn't take prenatal vitamins anyway, they made me sick. Finally getting some sleep, I was so annoyed when Ava woke me up to talk to Anthony. All I wanted to do was sleep. As soon as he hung up, it was like his baby was punishing me for not talking to his ass.

Laying on this bathroom floor, I figured it was easier to just stay here and sleep, so if I had to throw up, I'd already be here. I wondered if Ava would bring me a pillow. I hoped I'd get over this soon; I have my first appointment tomorrow. I hadn't told Anthony, and Ava was telling me I should. I can't stand her sometimes and her good heart. Anthony was just an asshole about her situation, but she still thinks I'm wrong for not telling him. I wish she would leave me alone.

"My, why you on the floor?" Hearing my husband's voice immediately annoyed me. Why is he here?

I didn't even bother answering him as I felt him moving around me. The next thing I know, I was being lifted off of the floor, into his arms. I wanted to fight against him, but I was honestly too tired to try. Strong, bright bitch.

He laid me on the bed and started undressing me. I let him care for me because I just couldn't fight in my weakness. After undressing me, he laid next to me and kissed my stomach. I still wanted to have an attitude, even with me being happy that I could feel him next to me.

"You might not want to lay in the bed. Ava slept with me last night, so you know, I don't want you to get AIDS," I sarcastically said, then tried to roll over on my side, but Anthony pulled me back so I couldn't roll.

"That's not what we are going to do, My. I was an asshole. There, I said it. I don't know a lot about the shit, so damn sue me." I still felt like that was an excuse.

"Oh, OK. I guess Google doesn't work for Anthony Montgomery." I chuckled.

"My, why would I randomly research AIDS?"

A streak of madness shot through me and I sat up and turned to him.

"She doesn't have AIDS, you dumb fuck! She has HIV, there is a damn difference." I hate when people do that, and to have it be my husband made it even worse. Anthony wiped his hand down his face in frustration.

"My, fuck! OK! I don't know shit about it, damn. You know I love Ava, and this doesn't change that shit. I guess I just need to get more educated about it. You can't blame me for not knowing; most people don't have knowledge about a lot of things until it becomes a need to know. I guess now I need to know.

I looked at him and thought about what he said. I guess he did have a point, but I was still in my feelings. I just wanted to talk to my best friend for a minute. Laying back down on the bed, I allowed him to pull me in his arms.

"I have my first appointment tomorrow."

Anthony looked at me and curved his lip. "Were you going to tell me if I didn't come over here? My, I know I said some messed up stuff and you mad, but, ma, please don't keep me from my baby or the growth of my baby."

I immediately felt guilty about not telling him about the appointment as soon as I made it. I did plan to tell him, though. "I was going to text you about the appointment later."

Feeling his hand slide down my stomach to my honeypot, I instantly felt the wetness between my legs. He kissed me on my neck and brought his mouth to my ear. I closed my eyes, awaiting his voice.

"I think you need some act right, Myah. You not about to keep me from my baby because we beefing." His finger going into my panties caused my legs to betray my mind and gap apart. Damn fingers whore. "Do you understand me, My?"

I moaned feeling his fingers in my folds and he kissed my

neck and gently bit it. He was always leaving marks on me. "Yes, I...I understand."

He was working his fingers like a master of everything right now and I couldn't think as my orgasm threatened to break me.

"Let that shit go, My, you need it. The faster you let it go, the faster I'm putting this dick in ya life."

That's all I had to hear. My gates came crashing open. I know Ava heard everything that went on for the next hour because we don't know how to be quiet when it comes to our sex. I love this man and we would work through this. I just prayed he truly meant what he said about getting educated because, husband or not, I would go to the wall for Ava.

ANTHONY AND I ENDED UP FALLING ASLEEP AFTER OUR make-up sex, and waking up the next morning in his arms felt right. My doctor's appointment was today, so I was getting up to start my day. It was still early, so I didn't bother waking Anthony; plus, I wanted to talk to Ava. Walking in the kitchen, Ava was sitting at her breakfast nook, drinking coffee or tea and reading the newspaper. Sometimes I think she is the only person that still gets physical newspapers. She said she likes the feel of the paper between her fingers. I'm a Kindle kind of girl. Ava has a massive library.

"Hey, pretty lady. How's your morning?" I asked as I fixed myself a cup of non-caffeinated tea.

Ava looked over the brim of her reading glasses and looked back at her paper. "It's going great. Especially after you and your husband left me out here with Isaac. No worries, though, he left shortly after what I think was your first orgasm."

I gasped at that news because I didn't know he came with Anthony. "Ava, I didn't know he was here."

She chuckled and got out of her seat and poured another cup of tea. "Anthony did, but it's cool. Nothing like being in the face of the man that thinks you're a nasty bitch. We didn't really talk, just sat there, looking awkward as hell. You still want me to go with you to the doctor, or is hubby back on his job?"

I felt like she had an attitude for some reason, and I wasn't sure why. "Ava, boo. Did I do something wrong? You seem a little snippy, and as for my husband, he was never off his job. I chose to block him from doing his job. Get right, Ava."

She looked at me with eyes that were hurt. "You're right and I apologize for that. You go ahead and handle your business with your hubby. Let me know what the doctor says."

She walked out of the kitchen as Anthony was walking in. They spoke to each other but it was clear she didn't want to. Anthony hugged me around my middle and kissed my neck.

"She OK?"

I turned to give him a kiss and just shook my head. I wasn't sure right now what she was, but I would talk to her later about it. Right now, it was about my husband and my baby.

We got to the doctor's office about fifteen minutes early so I could complete my paperwork. There were a few couples with newborns, and I was just in a lovey mood. I talked to all of them and one even let me hold their baby. I looked at Anthony and he looked so happy. I guess he really wanted this.

We waited for about twenty minutes before I was called to the back. They did a urine and blood pregnancy test. My doctor was the same I had when I was pregnant with AJ; well, he's actually been my doctor since I was a teenager. He was basically a part of my family, seeing as he is my father's battle buddy.

Anthony helped me get undressed when we got in the room and, of course, he was trying to be fresh. I swear he had no couth. I was just happy that he was happy, and although I was pushing back in the beginning, I really wanted this. Hearing a knock on the door, I was excited to see my doctor.

"Myah love! How are you?" Dr. Jakes asked as he gave me a hug. He then turned to dap Anthony. Dr. Jakes was the coolest white man I ever did meet. "Hey, Doc! It's been too long."

His smile was so bright. "So, I see you've been being grown. Congratulations, you two. I want to do an ultrasound just to check things out. I shouldn't have to do a vaginal at this point because, based on your bloodwork, you look to be about six weeks. Let's see what we have."

Anthony moved to my head and kissed my forehead. I looked up at him as he looked at the screen while the doctor moved the little thing around on my abdomen. There was a sparkle in his eyes, and I loved that.

"Here we go, see that little sweet pea right there? That's your baby. The size of a sweet pea. Everything is looking pretty good, Myah." He printed off about seven copies of the picture and handed them to Anthony. The wetness in his eyes let me know he wanted this more than even I knew. I sat up and wiped my belly off.

Dr. Jakes moved and stood back against the counter while I got myself together with Anthony's help. When we sat down, he started the conversation I didn't want to have.

"Myah and Anthony, I am excited about this new pregnancy, but I would not be a good doctor if I didn't address the previous. With everything that happened with that pregnancy, I will want to see you twice a month. I'm going to list you as high-risk and I will make sure I stay on you. Myah love, I need you to keep your stress level down.

This is now your uncle talking... I don't care what it is, Myah. If it's your job that's stressing you, I will sign for you to go out on a leave. We are going to have a healthy baby, Myah. I'll do my part, and I know Anthony will, but I need you to do yours. It's time to take care of you." He gave me a stern look and I nodded my head.

I knew where this talk was coming from. Dr. Jakes knows Ava the same as he knows me. Our fathers and him were in the same regiment. Jakes, as we called him, also knew Ava's status because he is her doctor. She started going to him when they decided they wanted a baby, which was months before she found out her status. He knew how stressed I was trying to be there for Ava after Andre died and just her well-being. Stress was a factor in my losing my son and I refused to let that happen again. I will definitely be there for her, but this time, I had to take care of me and mine. I had to come first.

Thirteen

Ava

I NEEDED TIME TO JUST BE ALONE AND RELAX. IT WAS Friday, so I decided to take the day to myself. Myah had been at my house for four days, and she was sick the entire time. I was so happy that she was pregnant and getting a second chance. When she lost AJ, I was just as devastated as she was because I blamed myself. Myah's heart is so big and she often puts others in front of herself. That is what happened when she was pregnant. I was in a horrible spot with Andre dying and me dealing with my diagnosis. There was a time that I wanted to die, and I stopped taking my meds, which caused my CD4 to drop below two hundred. When your CD4 drops below two hundred, you are classified as having AIDS. Myah came over and gave me a riot act and I went to my doctor to restart my antiretroviral therapy (ART). Within a month, my CD4 count was back up above two hundred.

Living with this has been hell and it's changed everything in my life. There was a time I wanted to start my own business, but the reality is, I have to be with a company with excellent health benefits. My treatment was not cheap and I wanted to live as long as possible. Thus far, I was doing great and I had been in an undetectable status for over a year now and I was proud of that. When a person reaches an undetectable level, that means their viral load is under a certain threshold. That threshold is twenty and my current viral load falls under that threshold. Undetectable does not mean I no longer have HIV, what it means is the viral load is so low that it cannot be measured on a test. It also means there is a ninety-two to ninety-six percent rate that I will not transmit the disease to others sexually if I am actively undergoing ART.

Myah knows all of this and that is her main reason for wanting me to date now. Even with knowing that information, I still just didn't want to be in the situation that I was now in. I really liked Isaac and his rejection of me hurt. It hurt more because he was rejecting me for something I had no control over. I didn't ask Andre to run a train on some girl so he would have practice to be ready for me. I most certainly didn't ask him to do it raw. Even with all of that, I loved him.

To find out your husband ran a train on a girl in college with his homeboys to have *practice* years after it happened is like a blow to everything you thought you knew. You go to the hospital thinking maybe he has the flu; oh, he does, but with a side of AIDS

I was by his side as I watched the pneumonia weaken him, and eventually, he died. Watching him deteriorate was the longest three months of my life. During that time, I had the time to forgive him. It took a lot of the Lord, but when my husband died, he died knowing I forgave and loved him. I would have never wanted him leaving the physical thinking that I held any type of hatred in my heart for him. I wanted him to rest peacefully.

I know most would think I should hate him, but I simply couldn't. Andre was a great husband to me. I had or have no doubt that he loved me, and yes, he made a tragic mistake that affected both of us, but I will not allow his love for me or my love for him to be negated.

Last night when Anthony came to get Myah, I never expected Isaac to be with him. It was the most awkward thing in the world. I didn't really know what to say to him, but he was so damn sexy, and I had come to the conclusion that he owned hundreds of grey and black sweatpants. Even though it was an off day for me at my own insistence, I decided I would still eat lunch at my favorite place, Aria.

Getting there, it was the same hostess that was there the day I came and had lunch with Isaac. I gave her a smile and she had a funny expression on her face. I really didn't understand why, however. Letting her know it was a table for one, she nodded her head and then we headed to my seat. Aria is generally packed for lunch and now was no different at all. When we got to what seemed to be the only seating in the restaurant, I understood the look on the hostess's face. Before me was Isaac sitting at a two-top table with a very beautiful woman. Based on her attire and flirtatious behavior, they looked to be on a date. I wondered if tomorrow was her day. He had yet to look up at me and I wanted to run out, but I was not going to give him that much power. I sat my pretty ass down at my table and pulled out my newspaper to finish my reading from this morning. As I read, I did discretely glance at him. I saw him look my way, and when he noticed it was me, I saw his demeanor change.

He was uncomfortable and I enjoyed that. I'm not sure why, but I did. I ordered my food, and when we made eye contact, I decided to be extra petty.

"Hey, Isaac! How are you?" He paused as if he didn't know whether to really speak or not. The female he was with turned and I admired her beauty. She looked to be a little older than him. I give it to Isaac, he had great taste.

"Hey...hey, Ava. You look good. How are you?" he asked with a slight smile. I smiled back and decided to just let the petty be great.

"Of course, I do. I mean, didn't I look great when you were at my house last night?" I gave a smirk and watched his eyebrow curve to my question.

He chuckled a bit before he responded to me. "Yeah, you did, ma. When I came through with Anthony to check on his wife, you damn sure looked good. Just as good as you did that weekend when I took you out."

Damn, he fired petty with petty and I don't think I was ready. I didn't really know what to say as he got up from the table with the female. He said something to her and then walked over to me.

"I see you on your petty game. Why, I'm not sure. I didn't do anything to you, ma. Anyway, I'll give my mom your apologies for your rudeness. Stay beautiful, baby girl." With that, he left me there feeling stupid.

I felt like in a matter of six days, everything was crumbling. I was hurt and rejected. This is an experience I'd never been through. I had been with Andre since my freshman year, so I never had to experience this. It just wasn't fair. I sat in my seat and felt the tears pooling, so I sat a fifty on the table and hurried out of the restaurant with tears falling from my eyes. When I exited the doors, of course, him and his mother were still standing directly in front of the restaurant talking. Yep, that's how the universe works! If I wasn't embarrassed enough, I had to endure the look of pity on their faces. I stood there for a second, wiped my face and held my head high as I walked my pretty ass off. I would not do this. I would not allow anyone to make me feel like I did something wrong by getting infected with HIV. Period.

IN THE PAST MONTH, I HAD BEEN SO BUSY. I WAS KEEPING myself busy and I had picked up a hobby of painting. Let me tell you, rejection will do something to you, especially when the rejection was not a fault of your own per se. That day, a month ago, when I ran into Isaac and his mother, I went to my hairstylist at Queen City Hair and told my girl Keema to cut it off. Of course, she told me no, so I took my happy tail to the bathroom with some scissors and helped her get a start. I thought her short ass was gonna fight me.

Now, my hair was short and honey blonde. No one had really seen it because I also decided to take a leave from work. Well, not a leave, but I had been working remote for the last month. I hadn't even seen Myah. I knew that upset her, but I told her it was time for her to focus on her family and I could take care of myself. With the guilt I felt from her losing her first baby, I would do everything in my power to not overwhelm her with me and my problem. I felt bad for staying away from Myah, but I needed this time, and so did she. I loved my cousin and wanted the best for her, and this was a part of that.

It was Saturday and I was sitting on my patio, just looking over the city. I loved my high-rise condo and the view. My patio wrapped around and it was amazing. There were only two apartments on my floor, each being twenty-five hundred square feet. My place was massive, and I loved it. I didn't have any kids, and clearly, it was looking like I wouldn't ever, so this was my oasis. Hearing my doorbell, I already knew it was Myah. She told me last night on the phone that she was coming by because she missed my face. Getting up to answer the door, I wasn't in a particular rush because I knew Myah was going to trip and I wasn't wrong.

"Let me find out! You done went and cut all you hair off

being grown!" See, dramatic. I just walked off from the door to go back to my patio. "And my baby got on pompom shorts."

"Myah, must you be so damn loud? I'm trying to relax." I didn't really want to be bothered. I knew she meant well, but at the end of the day, I was just chilling.

Myah stood in front of me, blocking my view, forcing me to look at her. "Look, bitch! I been nice long enough. Anthony told me to leave you alone, but it stops today and now. Get your ass up and come with me now. Don't play with me either because you know I'll fight your ass."

We had a stare off for a good two minutes before I just decided to go with her. Hell, I needed to get out of the house anyway and didn't want to move my car. "Whatever, bitch! Let me get my shoes."

I thought about changing my shorts but decided against it. I did put a sheer, long top over it, though. Getting in Myah's Lexus NX SUV, I reclined my chair and closed my eyes. I didn't realize I was tired until I was being shaken awake. Rubbing my eyes, I noticed we were at her house.

"Myah, why are we at your house? I don't want to go in there and have to force Anthony to disinfect it all after I leave."

Myah shot daggers at me with her eyes, but I really didn't care.

Her face softened before she addressed my shade. "Ava, please don't do that. I have talked to Anthony and he knows that he was wrong. At least allow him the right to apologize."

I didn't say anything as we got out the truck, but I took in what she said. When we walked in the house, I tried to walk back out, but she blocked me. They were having one of their usual weekend cookouts and I did not want to be around this many people. Looking over and seeing Isaac sitting at the card table, playing spades definitely made me want to leave.

"Myah, why would you do this?" I asked her in a low tone. I hadn't told her about what happened at Aria; again, I was embarrassed. Who wants to keep talking about rejection?

"Ava, you're a part of this family and I miss you. Please just come on." Myah pulled me into her arms and hugged me. I allowed my face to go into her shoulder because I was feeling my emotional wall breakdown. Feeling a tap on my shoulder, I turned to see Anthony standing there.

"Hey, sis. How you doing?"

I gave a small smile.

"I've been better, but hey, at least I'm here." As I spoke, I glanced to the card table and saw Isaac watching me. It felt uncomfortable, so I moved out of his view.

"Yeah, I'm happy you came. I wanted to apologize for that fuck shit I said. You know I love you, right?" I didn't say anything, but I did notice that he had yet to hug me. That was something he usually did immediately. I was tired of nitpicking about stuff, so I just told him yeah and excused myself to the bedroom.

I had to get away. I just couldn't be in the midst of all of this right now, so I did what I do best: ordered an Uber. I knew that Myah wasn't going to come in here because she was a give-her-space kind of girl. When my app alerted me that it was here, I quickly but cautiously exited the room. Before going to the living room, I looked around to see if Myah was in there, but I heard her in the kitchen, talking to someone. Once I knew I was in the clear, I headed to the door, but not before looking towards the card table. Isaac seemed to be watching my every move. I looked at him for a minute and I saw something in his eyes, but I didn't know what it was. I didn't have time to care because, right now, my only mission was to get the hell outta here.

Fourteen

I saac

I HAD NO IDEA WHAT WAS GOING ON WITH ME. I COULDN'T stop thinking about this damn girl. When we went to her house to get Myah, it was awkward as hell. I didn't know what the hell to say to her. I did the normal how you doing piece and she gave me a half-ass answer. She offered me a drink, then got smart with her mouth, talking about, *"Just warning you, I drank from all the glasses. Wouldn't want you to catch anything with me being the walking dead."* I wanted to choke her little ass out, but I decided to ignore her ass.

I sat there in silence while she moved around nervously, trying her best to ignore me. When I heard Anthony and Myah's loud ass, I decided to catch an Uber to his house to get my car to go home. I was so over this shit. I left her house without saying a word, but my mind felt like it stayed there because I couldn't stop thinking about her. Imagine my surprise, seeing her the very next day at Aria when I was with my mother. I mean, the last time I was there was the first time, but I liked it, so I told my mother then brought her. Based on the way Ava was dressed, I could tell she wasn't at work, but what I didn't expect was for her to be petty as hell. It was actually cute in its own way, but I would never tell her that.

When we left, my mother had a hundred questions about her. I didn't want to just disclose her status, so I just told her it didn't work out between us. I knew my mother knew there was more to that and she was about to call me out on it, but something halted both of our conversations: Ava coming out of the restaurant with tears streaming down her face. In my soul, I felt like I wanted to hug her, but I just stood there, looking at her, then something amazing happened. She found her magic. Ava wiped her face and lifted her head and walked by us like she wasn't just crying. I watched her walk until I couldn't see her anymore. What my mother said to me once I returned my gaze to her had been sitting on my chest since she said it.

My mother said, "A woman that can gather herself and her worth like that is a warrior. Son, I don't know why it didn't work, as you say, between you, but you need to figure it out. I guarantee you, she is what you need."

Under normal circumstances, I would agree with my mother, but I'm sure she wouldn't say that if she knew she had AIDS. I don't know how anyone can work something like that out.

IT HAD BEEN A MONTH SINCE ANYONE HAD SEEN AVA. Anthony told me that she talked to Myah everyday but wanted Myah to concentrate on having a calm pregnancy. I could tell he felt bad about the situation and I actually did, too. Ava was a beautiful girl and she was given a messed-up hand in life. I had been thinking about her a lot, but I just didn't know. Damn, why she had to have that shit? Myah had stopped really talking to me and I wasn't really sure why. I really didn't feel like I had done anything wrong. I never once disrespected Ava or told her business.

Anthony and Myah were having one of their usual cookouts that they often had. I have to admit; their cookouts were always on point. I don't really know if it counts that they had it catered, but the barbeque spot they used was amazing, so I was always going to be in attendance. Plus, it was the best place to come up on a lick. Dudes always think they can play Spades until they got on the table with me and Anthony. We always cleaned house and dudes was mad, especially since the pot minimum was a grand. Myah came over to the table and told Anthony she would be back in a minute, and like an overprotective husband and father, he asked a hundred questions. When she told him she was going to get Ava, I didn't know if I should leave.

She hadn't been around in a long time and I wasn't sure what was going on with her; hell, none of us did. He told me to chill because he was going to apologize to her for that disinfectant comment. When he told me he said that, even I was shocked, but neither of us really know anything about the disease, but I was taking a guess that it couldn't be transmitted like that. About an hour and a half later, the alarm alerted that Myah was coming in the door, making me look to it. When she walked in, I didn't even recognize the woman behind her. She tried to leave, but Myah pulled her in anyway. Damn! Ava had cut all her hair off and went blonde. The shit was sexy as fuck. I don't understand why I can't get this damn girl off my mind. I was trying my damn hardest. She had on these shorts that were sexy as hell. When she noticed me looking at her, she moved so I wouldn't be able to see her and that bothered me.

Anthony paused the game to go say something to her. It wasn't a long conversation, and when he came back, I wondered what was said.

"Yo, she good?" I asked Anthony, who responded with a head shake.

"Man, I feel like I fucked up our whole relationship by my reaction. I know she thinks I didn't want to hug her because I usually do, but I'm not sure what her mindset is right now." Anthony sounded bothered as hell and I understood why. Ava was like Anthony's little sister, and now they had a strain between them.

We continued to play the game. Myah was in the kitchen with some of the other ladies in the house while Ava had gone in the back of the house. Not even thirty minutes after she got here, I saw Ava looking like she was on some mission impossible shit, trying to sneak out the house. When she got near the door, we made eye contact. Her eyes were so sad and empty, and I hoped I wasn't a cause of that. When she walked out the door, all I could do was sigh at the turn of events.

Hours after the cookout ended, I was still there, lit as hell in Anthony's mancave. We were just chilling and going over the events of the cookout. There was this bad ass chick there that was on my dick, but I was hesitant. The situation with Ava made me have a little more pause about just randomly messing with chicks. I wanted to see chicks' most recent test results at this point in the game.

"Damn, lil' mama was on you, though. You gonna handle that?" Anthony inquired as he sipped on his cup.

"Bruh, I don't even know. A nigga not trying to have another chick wasting my time. Hoes out here do the most. Wasted damn near four months." We both chortled at my statement, but that ended when Myah came in, looking like she was about to commit murder.

"So, this is how we do it? Wait to get in private and talk

shit about my cousin who has never done anything to either of you niggas? Anthony, I see your ass hasn't learned your lesson quite yet. As much as I want to curse you stupid fuck niggas out, I'm going to take this time to educate you because clearly, y'all are the children that were left behind."

Myah wasn't yelling but she was scaring me. I rather her ass scream on me, but when she got a stool and sat in front of me and Anthony, I knew shit was real. I looked at Anthony and he looked like a damn five-year-old in trouble for spilling his juice.

"OK, kiddies. I want this lesson to be as interactive as possible. If I ask a question and you know the answer, make sure you raise your hand, OK!" Myah paused as if she was assessing our comprehension.

"Can anyone first tell me how Ava contracted HIV? I mean, since hoes do the most, let's explore that." I slightly dropped my head at her statement because I wasn't meaning to reference Ava as a hoe, but the way it sounded, I understood her offense. Anthony nor I said anything.

"OK, let's not forget to raise our hands if we know the answer. Well, let me tell you a story about a girl who met the love of her life her freshman year of college. Ava was a virgin when she met Andre, and so was Andre. They started dating shortly after they met because Ava is the bomb. Isaac, I think you know that, but anyway. Ava held out on sex with Andre because she wanted to make sure he was the one. Well, Andre's stupid friend convinced him that he needed practice, so he made the decision to participate in a train. Well, that one night of practice was the one night he would be infected with the virus. Now, like most black people, he only went to the doctor when he was sick, which was like never. His one-time stepping out on their relationship ended with him being infected and infecting my cousin. Crazy thing is, she didn't find out until he had full-blown AIDS." Myah paused, and I was sitting there in shock again.

So, Ava was blindsided with this shit. Damn! I couldn't imagine something like that happening to me.

"Does anyone know the difference between HIV and AIDS?" Myah paused once again, and this fool Anthony's hand shot up in the air. I looked at his ass with a full side-eye.

Myah pointed at Anthony. "Yes, Anthony."

"Yes, the difference is the CD4 count. AIDS CD4 count is less than two hundred, HIV count is above two hundred but less than five hundred. Normal count is five hundred or above. Right?" Anthony answered that shit with pride, and I had to give a low chuckle.

Myah's smile was so big, all I could do was shake my head at the two. "Very good, Anthony. I'll give you your prize tonight." She winked at him and this light bright nigga blushed.

"Yes, so to be clear, Ava has HIV, not AIDS. Don't make that mistake again, either of you. Now does anyone know what undetectable means?" I didn't know what that shit meant, so I just looked at her. I guess since Anthony didn't raise his hand, he didn't know, either.

"Well, gentlemen, especially Isaac, you will want to pay attention to this. There are two numbers that are commonly talked about when a person has HIV or AIDS and that is the CD4 count and the viral load. We already discussed the CD4 count, but for the viral load, that number can be in the hundreds of thousands, but if your viral load falls under a certain threshold, they deem you undetectable. That threshold is twenty." This new information sounded interesting, so it made me sit up. Myah curved her brow at me and continued.

"Does anyone want to take a guess what Ava's viral load

might be?" I looked at Anthony and felt silly as hell when I hesitantly raised my hand.

Myah's foolish ass hopped in her seat in excitement. "Oh, look! Isaac, yes!"

I shrugged my shoulder before voicing my thought. "Uuumm, less than the twenty-threshold requirement."

Myah jumped up and down, clapping her hands. "Yes! Isaac, you are right. Ava has been undetectable for over a year now. Now, so we are clear, with her being undetectable, there is a ninety-two to ninety-six percent chance that she will *not* transmit the virus to her partner as long as she is taking her antiretroviral therapy or ART as it is also called."

Now I was confused as hell. I never heard any of this about HIV "Wait, I'm confused, so she doesn't have HIV?"

Myah shook her head. "No, she still has HIV. The point of the Antiretroviral therapy or..."

"ART!" Anthony yelling out made me bust out laughing! This nigga was really in here like he was in class or some shit.

"That's right, babe! You gonna get it tonight!" Myah winked at him as she spoke, and his bright ass was red with excitement. I had no idea why I fool with these two.

Myah continued talking. "The point of ART is to bring that viral load down so it can be as low as possible. Ava adheres to her therapy, so she has been undetectable for a long while. Now, I've given you a lot of information and I implore you both, especially you, Isaac, since my cousin *really* likes you and is heartbroken that you look at her like a nasty bitch... Go do some research. Now your homework assignment is to look up what a PrEP drug is. Class, I am so proud of you!"

I looked at Myah and shook my head. It bothered me that she thought I looked at Ava like that. "Myah, I never looked at your cousin like a nasty bitch. Does she think that?"

Myah's eyes held a sadness that I didn't like. "Isaac, you do realize before Andre and after Andre, Ava has never been with another man. After her diagnosis, she felt unworthy of love and your rejection of her was a reinforcement of that feeling. I know that her having HIV is a big deal, but I also have done the research and she has done everything to mitigate the risk to a potential partner."

Myah's eyes watered and Anthony was at her before the first tear could fall. "I love Ava and I wish this hadn't happened to her. She is an amazing person who lives in a bubble because she feels no one will ever love her. That's why I never even told my husband. Anthony, you think it wasn't noticeable that you didn't hug her? She noticed and she left. I asked her to be my baby's godmother and she actually declined. My best friend declined! She didn't think you would want her to touch my baby!"

Myah was in a full cry now and I felt like less of a man. This was a lot to deal with, though, and I wasn't sure how I would.

I DECIDED TO EAT SUNDAY DINNER WITH MY PARENTS because I wanted to talk to them about my situation. I talk to my parents about almost everything going on in my life and this Ava situation was going to be no different. My mother had already been asking about her since we saw her at the restaurant, she just doesn't know that she was Ava. I couldn't get Ava off my mind and that was bothering me, but since last night, and getting the new information from Myah, my interest piqued. When I got home, I did some research, and sure enough, Myah spoke truth. It was crazy how much information was out there to find, and it definitely had my interest.

My mom had thrown down, as always, cooking a banging

ass pot roast stuffed with potatoes and veggies, macaroni and cheese and cornbread. I had two plates before I decided to engage in a conversation about what I really wanted to talk about.

"Ma, you remember the girl I told you about who was hot and cold with me?" I jogged her memory with my question.

"Yeah, son, the one who was stuck on her deceased husband, right?"

I gave a light laugh at the mention of her husband. I definitely don't think she was stuck on him, but that's another topic.

"Well, yeah, kinda. Well, you remember the girl from the restaurant? That's the same girl." My mother tilted her head and I knew I had her attention.

"Well, son. What was the problem? I heard her say you were at her house and you took her out. Why didn't y'all work out?" my mom asked me, and I took a minute to look at my father, who was quietly invested in the conversation but I knew he wouldn't speak on anything until he was ready.

"Ma, well uumm...she told me...uummm..."

My father sucked his teeth. "Boy, spit it out."

"She told me she was HIV positive."

My mother's eyes bugged out a little bit and she sat back in her chair. My father lowered his head and shook it at the news.

"Wow, now that is something I didn't expect you to say. Did she contract if from her husband?"

I nodded my head to answer the question nonverbally.

"Wow, son. Well, what is her status? Is she undetectable?" Now that made me sit up in my seat. I just learned about this last night, so I was shocked that she knew about this.

"Ma, how the hell you know about that undetectable stuff? I just learned last night after Myah petty ass took me and Anthony to school." I wanted to know how she had information I didn't know.

"Son, one of my good friends is HIV positive, so I know a lot, and so does your father. When someone you love most is affected by this virus, you learn everything you can to keep yourself safe and them here with you for as long as possible. Now what is her status?" My mother was straight to the point.

I shifted in my seat before giving her the information she was seeking. "Myah said she's been undetectable for over a year now and she is adhering to her ART."

My mother smiled and nodded her head. "You don't want to get involved with her because of the virus?"

I looked at my mother with crazy eyes. "Of course, I don't. Ma! I want to be with someone I can actually have sex and children with."

My mother laughed and my father even chuckled. My father must have decided it was time to speak. "Son, have you researched what PrEP drugs are?"

That is something I had yet to do. I had completely forgotten that Myah told us that was our homework. I told my father I hadn't.

"Son, PrEP is a way for people who don't have HIV but are at a substantial risk of getting it, I.e. being in a relationship with a person infected, can avoid becoming infected by taking the meds every day. It's kinda like birth control but it can save your life. With Ava adhering to her therapy, being undetectable, and if you take the meds, your chances of getting infected are in fact slim to none. Oh, and being infected does not make you infertile. Our infected friend is not only happily married to a person that is not infected, but they also have four children who are also not infected." My father paused for my response.

I was floored about the information I was getting. I really

didn't know a lot about this, and I wanted to know. I mean, I can't lie and say I wasn't feeling Ma because I was. I sat there in a small daze because I didn't really know how to feel. Feeling my mother touch my hand brought my mind back into the room.

"Son, I know your heart is torn. I get it! What man wants to be with the girl with HIV? I'll tell you this, son, and the only reason I am telling you this is because I want you to get a full scope of this. Your Uncle Mase is that man."

My mouth dropped open. My Uncle Mase was my favorite uncle and his wife, Marci, was my favorite aunt. They had been together for like fourteen years.

"Auntie Marci has HIV?"

My father nodded his head. "Yes, she does. She was infected by rape about two years before meeting Mase. This was back when there was even way less knowledge, research or advancement in the treatment. I'm not saying it was easy for them, but that man loves her. He is not infected and gets tested every three months. Your cousins are healthy as an ox and not infected. Son, all we're saying is her being infected is not a good enough reason to write her off."

My parents had given me a lot to think about, and now knowing that my Auntie Marci was positive changed my outlook. Could I be in a relationship with Ava, knowing she positive, or would it be too much? I mean, it's not like she wears a sign that gives her status. Hell, I didn't even know she had it, so why would anyone else think she did? Damn, I got a lot to think about.

Ava

BEING BACK IN THE OFFICE WAS TAXING BECAUSE I REALLY didn't want to be here. If it wasn't for me being over this campaign, I would definitely take a real leave of absence. I just wanted to go away somewhere. Although I fussed about the cost of the trip to the Maldives, I wanted to go again. I just wanted to stay in another overwater bungalow. That's when it dawned on me that I remembered seeing the same type of spots on an advertisement about Jamaica. Getting my laptop, I looked it up and found exactly what I was looking for. I decided I would take a solo vacation in three months. I didn't plan to tell anyone about my vacation because sometimes, being alone was good for the soul. Plus, I knew if I told Myah, she would want to tag along. I just didn't want to have to tell her no because I would this time.

I loved watching the sun set from my patio and I made sure I was always home in time to see it. A glass of wine, my thoughts and the sun. I thought about everything that had happened in the last few months. From Isaac pursuing me with a passion to him now staying away from me with that same energy. I hated that I had to live with this virus, but I just was not in a space in life that I would allow anyone to make me feel less than. I do a great job of making myself feel less than, I don't need any damn help. A part of the reason I always made sure I was on point is because I don't want anyone to even have an inkling that I could be sick. I never wanted anyone at my job to know or anywhere for that matter. Outside of my doctors, the only people that knew were Myah, my parents and now her husband and Isaac. This is not something you bring up in casual conversation and I kept my circle tight. By tight, I meant Myah.

Sipping on my glass of wine as I laid on my patio lounge chair wrapped in my throw, I thought about sleeping out here tonight. It's something I did sometimes. I had a screen that could roll down the entire length of my patio that Anthony installed when I bought the condo. Just as I was dozing off, my doorbell rang, and I was immediately annoyed. Why can't Myah keep her pregnant ass home? Pulling myself out of my comfortability, I made my way to the door, still holding my glass of wine and wrapped in my blanket. Pulling the door open, I almost dropped my damn glass.

"Isaac, what are you doing here?" I heard the crack in my own voice as he stood before me, looking like heaven on earth in yet another pair of sweatpants. God is going to stop playing with me.

"Hey, Ava. I wanted to talk to you. I know I should have maybe called; well, I did, but it seems like you blocked my number."

I let my eyes drift so that we were no longer making eye contact out of guilt. I had blocked him a while ago on some forget him movement.

I decided to not even address that. I was interested in what this was about. "Yeah, sure, we can talk. Come in."

I moved to the side and let him in, taking in his natural scent. I directed him to the living room, and he sat down. It was clear that he was uncomfortable, so I offered him a bottle of water and he actually accepted. When I handed him the bottle, our hands touched, and I felt the spark that I felt before and it saddened me. I allowed him to take a sip of his drink and get to his comfortable place so he could start this conversation. I was sitting across from him in my oversized single chair, still wrapped in my blanket.

"I wanted to come talk to you about...uumm...about what you told me." He didn't even want to say the words.

"You want to talk to me about being HIV positive?" I wanted to be sure that was what he wanted to talk about because, at the end of the day, I had told him a lot of stuff.

"Yes, Ava. I wanted to talk to you about that. Well, since you told me and I had a discussion with Myah, I decided to do some research."

Now that made me sit up in my seat.

"OK, research is a good thing, I guess. What was it that you found in your research?" I wondered where this conversation would end.

He moved a little in his seat, then looked at me with a questionable gaze. "Myah told me that you were undetectable. Is that right?"

I nodded my head in confirmation. "Well, I was doing some, you know, research. I don't know, like, I really like you, Ava, but it's just..."

I already knew what he was thinking without him even having to say it. "I know, how do you be with someone who is HIV positive? Isaac, I don't know how to answer that for you. This is a first-time experience for me, too. I didn't ask for this, but I have to have faith that God has someone out there just for me. I may not deserve it, but I want it."

Isaac lowered his head for a moment before he continued. "I found out a few days ago that my favorite auntie is positive; her and my uncle have been married for fourteen years with four kids."

"Oh, wow. She had her children after her diagnosis?" I was surprised to hear this information.

"Yeah, she was infected two years prior to meeting my uncle. Anyway, finding that out made me kind of have a different outlook, so I had a sit down with my uncle, you know, man talk." Isaac's chuckle made me smile a bit.

"Oh, OK. Well, I'm sorry to hear about your auntie, but if that sparked your interest to do research, I'm happy about that. It's important to know how to keep yourself safe when it comes to the people you love."

It warmed my heart to hear that his auntie had four kids after her diagnosis. It gave me hope, but as soon as I got the hope, it left. I had to have a man to have a baby.

Isaac smiled at me, then what he said gave me pause. "Well, actually, finding out about my auntie didn't spark my interest, my interest in you sparked my interest. Ava, I like you a lot, but I just don't know as a man how to navigate this shit. I have to be honest."

I sat there, not really knowing how to feel or even what to say. I wanted Isaac and I felt like he was trying to say he wanted me, too, but just didn't know how to have me. I sat there and looked at him. Could he really want me, even with this? As I sat there and we looked at each other almost aimlessly, an idea popped in my head.

"Isaac, how about this? I'll make an appointment with my doctor and we can sit down with him. He can answer any question you have about the virus, me and how to keep you safe if you were to ever decide you wanted to be with me."

Isaac seemed to be in thought before agreeing to that idea.

I told him I would make the appointment and he stood to leave. Once we were at the door, we said our goodbyes and Isaac reached out and pulled me in for a hug. I'm not sure why, but it made me emotional. I was sure he wouldn't want to touch me, but him initiating it meant more than he would ever know. That sense of rejection was fading away slowly.

I MADE THE APPOINTMENT FOR THE NEXT WEEK AND I unblocked Isaac and texted him the information. Isaac texted me during the rest of the week and we spoke a little that way, but he didn't call. I was just happy to even have communication with him again. My appointment was in the morning and I was nervous, but Myah was at my place, calming my nerves.

"Ava, the fact that he even came over here says a lot. I knew my little schoolhouse special would enlighten him." Myah seemed proud of herself, and all I could do was shake my head.

"I know and thank you for your lesson. I think it was more of him finding out his favorite auntie was positive, though," I let her know with a giggle. The look she gave me made me laugh harder.

"So, you're just going to disregard my hard work and lesson I gave to my husband and your future husband? I always knew you were a damn hater."

I couldn't stop laughing at her because she was so serious.

"Girl, why are you so silly, and future husband? Yeah, I don't think so."

No matter how bad I wanted Isaac, I wasn't foolish enough to believe that he would stick around.

Myah gave me a full smirk. "OK, when y'all are getting married and having babies, remember I called it."

I didn't even bother to verbally respond. I had enough stuff on my mind to worry about Myah's pipe dreams for my life. I was nervous just thinking about tomorrow and the fact that Isaac would be hearing intimate details of my life and health. I really do appreciate him for even wanting to know because it is more than I expected.

Isaac and I agreed to meet at my doctor's office. I was pleased to see that he was already there when I pulled into the parking lot. He got out of his car before I did, and I was shocked he didn't have on sweatpants. He was dressed in a pair of dark denim jeans, J's, and a Black By Popular Demand Jersey Shirt. This man is just a blessing and he doesn't even know it. I was nervous because I decided to wear a pair of distressed jeans to match my feelings in the moment and a shirt that read Fuck-Boy Free The Glo Up on it. It was a crop top to be exact that hung off my shoulder and I paired it with some Vans. My shortened hair was curly because I decided on a wash and go. I looked completely different than any other time Isaac had ever seen me.

Walking up to him as he leaned on his Range Rover, I took it in because I'd been thinking about purchasing one but wasn't sure. Isaac had a smirk on his face, but I wasn't really sure why.

I tried to break the ice with, "I like your Range. I've been thinking about getting one myself."

Isaac leaned off of his truck, grabbed my hand and pulled me into him for a hug. I smiled because this was now the second time he had touched me after knowing my status. A lot of times when people find out, they try to avoid touching me as if that is a way to transmit the virus.

"I like your shirt...so you fuck-boy free?" I gave him a blushing smile because I really didn't know how to answer the question. I'll just take it as a rhetorical. I let him know we could go in since the appointment I set was in about ten minutes. We walked into the office and was greeted by Janice, the receptionist. She knew why I was here and that was why she immediately ushered us to the back to a consultation room.

We sat in the room and I shifted in my seat uncomfortably; well, that was until I felt his hand on my knee, causing me to look his way. "Chill out, Ava. I'm here, right?"

I didn't really know what that meant, but for right now, I wouldn't worry about it. My Doctor, Dr. James Thomas, walked in the room with a smile on his face. Yes, Dr. Thomas is the same doctor who broke the news of my status as well as my husband's all those years ago. Who knew that he was one of the leading doctors on the topic of HIV and AIDS. Apparently, once the test results came back for Andre, they sought him out as his office was in the hospital to come and talk to us. He has been with me every step of this journey, and sometimes, I think his faith willed me to live on.

"Hi, Ava. How are you today?" I stood and gave him a hug. Dr. Thomas was an older man, but he was fine as hell. If he was interested in women, I would definitely throw all this snatch at him. I don't think his husband would approve, however.

"I'm amazing, Dr. Thomas. Ummm, this is Isaac." I didn't want to allude to our connection because I honestly didn't know what our connection was. Isaac stood and greeted the doctor, then we all took a seat.

"Well, Ava, based on our conversation, Isaac here may have some questions about HIV as it pertains directly to you. Is that right?" Dr. Thomas faced Isaac, awaiting a response.

Isaac straightened his back and rubbed his hand down his beard. "Yeah, I guess you can say that. This is a new type of situation for me and I am just trying to see if it's something that I can navigate. I mean...I don't know."

Dr. Thomas smiled. "Isaac, the only way this conversation will work is if you are open and honest. I understand this can be a touchy situation, believe me. My husband of many years is HIV positive, so believe me, I understand your reservations and I'm a doctor that specializes in the field."

Watching Isaac's face etch in confusion, caused me confusion. "Wait, can you just tell that man's status like that? Isn't that like a HIPAA violation or some shit?"

Both me and Dr. Thomas laughed before he answered. "Well, I guess it would be if my partner didn't give me permission to share it to assist couples like you."

I felt uncomfortable with him thinking we were a couple, so I quickly spoke up to correct it. "No, Dr. Thomas, we aren't a couple."

"Ava, him being here says a lot. I'm a man regardless of my sexuality, and if he's here, he very much is thinking of being with you. Am I wrong?" I looked at Isaac for confirmation and him nodding his head was confirmation enough.

"So, let's get into it, shall we?" Dr. Thomas asked.

For the next hour, we discussed everything around my diagnosis and how Isaac could very much be in a normal relationship and still be safe from being infected. We talked about the riskier sexual activities such as anal. I think he was most happy to hear that there was no risk in me giving him head because he's not positive and even him giving me head was OK because research shows there is not a single case where a woman has transmitted to a sexual partner from receiving oral. We talked about the potential of me having a perfectly healthy baby even with my status.

The conversation proved to be informative and Isaac even left with a prescription for Truvada, which is a Pre-exposure Prophylaxis (PrEP) drug when taken once a day orally will reduce HIV infection risk. He was also tested today and would be every three months. That combined with my undetectable status and adherence to my antiretroviral therapy was all a nice formula to be with me and have a sexual relationship without the fear of being infected.

I wasn't sure what any of this really meant, but Isaac wanting to sit down with me at dinner tonight was a good sign, I guess. I wondered if God could have really put someone here just for me even in my circumstance, or would this be a sweet rejection.

Sixteen

I saac

I HAD BEEN ON INFORMATION OVERLOAD FOR ALMOST A week. With the research that I had chosen to do on my own about the virus and talking to Myah, my parents and my auntie and uncle, there was so much I just didn't know. My auntie is also undetectable, and my uncle takes Truvada and had been for a long time now. It was extremely uncomfortable asking my auntie and uncle about their sex life, but it was a necessary evil if I really wanted to consider things with Ava. I just couldn't be in a relationship with a woman if I couldn't get my dick wet. It just is what it is. Ava was fine and all of that, but nah, I was good if I couldn't slide in her.

My uncle let me know that him and his wife rarely use protection, but if they engage in risky sex, like anal, they do. That was way too much information for me, and knowing how my uncle and auntie get down in the bedroom made me feel like I was a young kid. I wanted to legit cover my ears. They had four children, a set of ten-year-old twins, a six-year-old and an eight-month-old. My uncle said the last one was a, *damn, she looks good in them jeans* baby. That made me laugh. My explained that his wife having the virus was not the hard part of the situation. The hard part was getting past his own thoughts and what he thought everyone else would think. He let me know at some point you have to forget about what everyone else thinks or says and just live life for yourself and your happiness.

That was the mindset I had when I knocked on Ava's door. I wanted to know more, and I was just going to have to man up and get the information I needed to make a well-informed decision on how I wanted to move forward. When she suggested sitting down with her doctor, I was thankful that she was open. Her doctor gave me a lot of information and basically confirmed the research I had done. I was very pleased that if I did proceed, we could still have an active sex life that included head on both of our parts. I'm not saying sex is everything in a relationship, but you'd be a fool if you said it wasn't important. Well, at least for a man like me. After we left the doctor's office, I set a dinner date with Ava and went to fill my Truvada prescription. Based on how this conversation went tonight, it would determine if I took the first of pills that I may be taking for a long time.

❧

I DECIDED TO TAKE AVA TO THE CAPITAL GRILLE FOR dinner. I would always try to make Ava feel special even if it were just in a friendship capacity. She told me that she would meet me there, which I expected, but what I wasn't expecting was how damn good she was going to look when she came through the door. Her haircut gave her this edge she didn't have before and I loved it. She had on a little black dress that went down to her calf and fit her like a glove. Getting up to greet her as she came to the table, I made sure to wrap my arms around her. She still felt right in my arms.

Helping her in her seat, I told her just how beautiful she was. We chit-chatted over our appetizers about trivial things, but when we were about ten minutes into the main course, I decided to broach why we were here.

"Well, today was really informative and I appreciate you allowing me to come with you."

Her smile was beautiful, and I would love to see it more often.

"I appreciate you for wanting to know. I mean, I know my circumstance is not an easy one, but I have to keep the faith that God has a greater plan for my life and that plan includes love. Everyone deserves love..." Her sentence faded off and there was a sadness in her eyes that I wanted to take away.

I shifted in my seat and reached across the table to grab her hand. "Ava, I really like you and I'm not saying this is not going to be hard. I mean, I never thought I would be interested in someone..."

"Never thought you would be interested in someone with a positive status. Yeah, well, I never thought I would have a positive status. Do you know I was the ideal girlfriend and wife? I never even looked at another man and let me tell you incase it's not clear: I'm a bad ass chick. Did you know I have never had sex with any other man outside of my late husband? He's been gone for five years. *Five years*! I haven't had sex in five years, not because I didn't want to but because I have this thing that makes people look at me like I am a nasty bitch. Kind of the same way you first looked at me when I told you. You remember, you asked me if I was a hoe or something." She gave a light chuckle but the tears in her eyes let me know she was not amused.

"Isaac, I want to be loved, held, cherished. I want a man to take me and love me just because, not in spite of. I want babies, I want to be married; hell, I want a man to fuck the common sense out of me."

Now that made my big mans jump in my slacks.

I had to let her hand go and readjust myself. "Ava, look, I'm going to be honest. I know this will take some navigating, but I want to try and be that man. I can't get your little ass out of my mind."

She let her tears fall freely from her face. I was very strategic in getting a private room for our dinner because I wanted us to be able to talk freely without her having a fear of extra ears. Getting up from my seat, I moved next to her seat and pulled her chair back, turning it around. Before squatting to her seated height, I moved the Truvada prescription out of my pocket and sat it on the table. She turned her head and looked at the prescription. Her tears increased as she picked it up.

"You...you filled it?" There was disbelief in her tone, and I guess I understood why. I didn't give her a vocal answer; instead, I took the bottle out of her hand. Once I had the bottle open, I took one pill out as the instructions read. I popped the pill in my mouth and grabbed the water to help it pass through my throat.

Ava's tears and smile made me smile. Taking her face in my hands, I pulled her down to my lips and gave her the kiss I'd been wanting to give her. Feeling her tears on my face, I knew she was still crying, and I confirmed once I pulled away.

"Ava, can we give this a shot?"

She nodded her head as she let her tears flow and I sealed our deal with one final kiss. I knew that this was going to be a journey, but it was one I was willing to take. After hours of conversations and research, I knew the risk and I had what was needed to mitigate it. I was going to give this a real shot because, at the end of the day, I had to live my life for me and my happiness.

෧෨

For the last two months, I have not had a day that wasn't spent with Ava. She is amazing and she had this way of making me feel like a true king. It wasn't a show of weakness on her part because she damn sure didn't let me get away with shit, but the strength on her made me stronger. I had been taking my one a day pill and it was like second nature now. We still haven't had sex yet and that was more me than her. She had sucked me off...a lot, and I felt bad as hell. There was still a hesitation when it came to full intercourse. Certain things that she does makes me think that she thinks I'm fucking with someone else. My babe sucked my dick literally at least twice a day, and trust me, I was thankful, but I could tell she is doing it more for me to be satisfied since we hadn't moved to sex.

I went and sat with my uncle and asked him if there was a hesitation when he first got with Auntie and he said there was. Again, I had to get out of my own head and just love her, it would all fall in place once I did. I felt like I loved her; hell, I definitely wouldn't be here if there wasn't love. Ava had this thing where she loved watching the sun set; she literally would be home in time for it every day. I tried to be there but missed it sometimes. Today, I told her I had late meetings but that was a lie. I wanted to surprise her and watch the sun set with her. We had exchanged house keys about a month ago, so I didn't announce myself as I entered. I was thinking about going to the Louries to get her security system together because it bothered me that she didn't have one.

I brought her a bouquet of pink and white roses; my baby loved fresh flowers. Walking deeper in the house, I knew she was on her patio because the sun was going to be setting soon. Before walking out of the already opened door, I stopped to listen to her conversation that she had on speaker-phone. I knew she was talking to Myah's loud ass because Ava don't fuck with anybody but her.

"Myah, he won't have sex with me. I know he's having sex with someone else. I mean, I suck him off a lot, but damn, I feel like why be with me if you're not sexually attracted to me?"

"Ava, girl, you're tripping. Y'all haven't been together that long. This is a difficult situation and I won't act like it isn't, so give him time. You know he wants you."

"I just feel alone still. I wish I could just die and be with Andre. Hell, at least in Heaven he'd fuck me. If this is what a relationship will be like with this shit I didn't ask for, then I just don't want to be bothered. I just want to sleep forever."

"Ava! I swear to God! I will come over there and slap you. You will not talk like that."

"Calm down, it's just a figure of speech."

"Your past does not allow you to use that as a figure of speech. I love you, Ava, and my baby needs his godmother."

"His? OMG! When did you find out?"

"Today, but I'm not telling Anthony yet. Girl, your sun is about to set so watch it and get yourself together before Isaac gets there."

"Ha, he won't be here 'til late. He said he had a meeting, but I guess his pussy was free. It is what it is. I think I don't care anymore, maybe this is my punishment for being stupid and loving hard."

"Ava, you are a blessing and trust me even if it's not Isaac, I promise he's out there."

I stood there frozen by what I just heard and stepped back to the kitchen. I needed a second to get it together. Damn. She really thought I was fucking with someone else. I suspected she did, but to hear her say it was a different feel-ing. Hearing her say she wanted to die hurt. I was her man and I was making her feel insignificant and that was not now or ever my intent. I took a minute and allowed the sun to set before I made my presence known by going out to the patio. Ava hearing me turned quickly in her seat.

"Babe! You scared me. What are you doing here?" Her smile was beautiful, but I realized in that moment that it didn't reach her eyes and that bothered me. She got up to greet me as she always did.

"I canceled my meeting so I could spend time with my babe."

I looked in her eyes and I saw the doubt. I gave her a kiss and let her suck on my tongue like she always did. Ava turned me on like fuck, and even in this minute, I had to calm my big mans down. When she reached down and rubbed him, I knew what she was about to do.

Like clockwork, she began to lower her body, but I stopped her.

"Nah, bae! I just want to chill tonight."

She shifted on her feet and dropped her arms from around my waist. "Oh, okay. Well, let me see what I can order in. I haven't really gone grocery shopping."

She didn't give me a chance to say anything more before she moved around me. Letting my head fall, I felt stuck. I didn't want her to feel like this. I turned to go in the kitchen, but she wasn't in there when I got there. Walking to the back of her condo, I heard the water running in the bathroom behind the closed door. I walked to the door and heard sniffles and that shit was a no-go for me. I stood right in front of the door like a wall. When she finally opened the door, she jumped.

"Damn, what is it Scare Ava day? Move, boy." She tried to push past me, but again, I was a wall. She looked up at me and her eyes were red.

"Why were you crying?" I was not going to play with Ava

today. I had been handling our entire relationship with kid gloves, but now I needed to man up.

"I...I wasn't. I had something in my eye."

She tried to laugh it off, but that shit was not working.

"So, we lying to each other now?"

She sucked her teeth to my statement and placed her hands on her hip as if she were intimidating in the least.

"Isaac, whatever. I lie, you lie, everyone lies." With a hard push, I allowed her to move me so she could come out of the bathroom. She had just pissed me off because a nigga like me had never lied to her.

Following her into the kitchen, I wanted this shit addressed. "I don't lie to your ass, ma. Get that shit right. Now why are you lying?"

When she turned to face me, there was a mixture of anger and hurt. "Isaac, why haven't we had sex yet?"

Damn, I didn't think she was going to ask me straight out. "Ma, I don't know. I'm not thinking about sex like that. We still getting to know each other."

Her laugh made me tilt my head. "Well, congratulations, Isaac. You just told your first lie. Did you forget you courted me before I told you my status? We talked on the phone about everything for almost four months, so try again. It's cool, I get it. You don't want to have sex with the HIV girl. Not really sure why you're wasting my time. I could be waiting for who will."

I don't know why but that shit rubbed me the wrong way, completely. "Word, like that, Ava? You waiting for someone who will fuck? Well, you might be waiting a while, ma. I'm here, I told you shit wasn't gonna be easy but I'm trying. I'm here even with your situation. Why can't you see that?"

Ava's head dropped, and when it lifted, the tears were there. "Isaac, I think we should just stop pretending. I don't want you to be with me because you think no one else will want me. I want you to be with me because you love me. Just because, not in spite of. So, I'd rather wait that while. I will not let you make me feel like I have no options. If that's the way you feel, fuck you. Wait, you won't. You can leave."

I stood there looking at her take her stand and it's like a lightbulb went off. I loved her. My mother told me she was a warrior, and in this moment, she wore all of her armor. My words were inconsiderate and filled with anger, but damn, this was a lot. I watched her move around me and towards the door. She opened her front door and stood there. I walked to the door and stood in front of her. I looked down at her and she wouldn't look at me.

With a softened voice, I tried to talk to her. "Ava. Babe."

"No, Isaac, you said what you meant, and with that, you can leave. Thank you for giving it a try, though."

I just watched her and knew no matter what I said, it wouldn't be received, so I decided to leave it there for right now. This shit wasn't the end so she could think what she wanted. I knew this was all new to both of us, but running at the first sign of trouble wouldn't be our thing. I was going to pull myself together and come back ready for Ava's ass. She better be ready, too.

Seventeen

M yah

AT TWENTY-TWO WEEKS, I WAS SO HAPPY I WAS PAST THE
morning sickness part of my pregnancy. Now I was in the big-
as-hell stage and Anthony's ass was getting on my entire
nerves. The closer I got to the timeframe when I lost AJ, the
more overbearing he became. This man got mad at me
because I woke up in the middle of the night to fix a grilled
cheese and egg sandwich. He had taken damn near everything
good out of the house and replaced it with some organic
substitute. Be clear, Little Debbie cakes don't have a damn
substitute. When I pounced on him like a spider monkey
after he threw out my Zebra Cakes, I bet his ass didn't touch
another Little Debbie cake I bought. I hadn't told him what
we were having because I was having a gender reveal today.

Ava had been helping me plan and I was so excited to be
sharing this with her. I had intentionally been keeping her
close to me since her little break from Isaac. Well, she was
taking a break, but Isaac made it clear to me and anyone who

would listen that she was his woman. Even though they were going through their little spat, I knew she missed him; hell, it had been three weeks. He was going to be here today, and I told her if she didn't show up because of him, I was disowning her. I wanted the gender reveal to be more of a cookout, chill thing so all of the men were responsible for gifting pampers and the women would go based on a registry.

"Myah, you think you have enough food? And why is there a platter of damn Zebra Cakes?" I had to pause from stirring the meatballs in the crockpot to side-eye her. She knows good and well that small platter was mine. When she started laughing, I knew she was being petty.

"Don't play with me, Ava. On another note, you look cute today. Let me find out you trying to make Isaac jealous with ya ass hanging out those shorts and that little ass crop top." Ava's body had always been stacked, and with the weather still being warm, she was showing her ass, literally.

She rubbed her hand down her ass and cuffed her bottom. "I'm not even thinking about that man. Plus, he's seen me in shorts before."

"I can promise you, he has *never* seen you in those little ass shorts. We'll see when everyone gets here, Ava. Don't get snatched because I'm going to laugh." I moved around the kitchen and took things out into the den and family room. I was not going to play with Ava.

About an hour later, the party was in full swing. Anthony was all over me and I didn't mind. He was like this when I was pregnant with AJ and I was so happy that he made me feel beautiful even though I felt big as hell. Isaac had arrived and I saw him pull Ava to the side. He did not look happy, but I told her about those damn shorts.

Anthony wrapped his arms around me and moved his lips to my ear. "Come with me to the bathroom, bae. I gotta show you something."

Turning around, I saw the mischievous look in his eye. "What you have to show me?"

He didn't answer as he pulled me to the hallway bathroom. Once we were in the bathroom, his lips landed on mine and his hands lifted my dress.

"Anthony, we have a house full of people, including my parents. What are you doing?"

Even though I was asking questions, I definitely wasn't stopping him from doing what he was doing. I needed it just as bad as he was trying to give it to me.

"My, I haven't been in this since the day before yesterday. Bend over so Daddy can get his dick wet before I go out here and fuck these niggas up on this spades table with Isaac." He didn't have to tell me twice; again, I wasn't trying to stop him.

I bent over, placing one foot on the closed toilet lid and my hands on the tub. Anthony lifted my dress over my hips, and I felt his lips on my ass cheek. With a kiss and a bite, I moaned from the pleasurable pain. Feeling his fingers in my folds made me shiver.

"Damn, you always wet for me, Myah, and it better forever be only me. Ya shit better prune up around other niggas." I had to laugh at him, but that laughter halted when he slid in with a death stroke. How is your first stroke a death stroke?

"Anthony, babe!" His strokes were so deliberate, and I was lost in them. I loved this man with the very being of who I was.

"You feel me, My? You feel me loving what's mine forever? Thank you, My. Thank you for giving me another baby. I love you." His affirmation of love made me emotional and I couldn't stop the tears.

Feeling my orgasm rise, I stiffened my back. "Nah, My, loosen that back before my baby kick the fuck outta you and I have to pop ya stomach."

As Anthony rubbed the arch in my back, I laughed because my son cuts up when we have sex and Anthony's ignorant ass pops my stomach, talking about he's not gonna be a cockblocker from the womb, I won't have it. I die laughing every time it happens. At the same time that my orgasm ripped through me, my son started kicking me and Anthony got to popping. I swear I love this man's foolish ass. It didn't take long for him to come to his orgasmic end after I used my vice grip between my legs. He took the time to clean me up while I caught my breath and I watched him as he cleaned himself.

"Stop looking at me like that, My, we'll be in here for another round." I laughed but got up to get out of the bathroom because I knew he was telling the truth. Walking out of the bathroom, I ran into my mother.

"Oh, sorry, Mama." She looked at me and shook her head.

"I told you not to get pregnant, now look at you, fat and shit. You should have took it as a sign when ya last one died."

I couldn't even think. Usually, my mother didn't address me like this in front of people. She generally played the doting mother in front of people, but today, she had been rude to me and I was confused. Anthony was still in the bathroom and I hoped he didn't hear her.

"Mama, why would you say that? My baby is a blessing. Daddy is happy that I'm giving him a grandbaby, why aren't you?" I was all but pleading for her to just accept me.

"Girl, fuck your daddy and that bitch he's with. Did you know he had a new woman? Who am I kidding, of course, you knew. You've always been on his dick with ya fat ass."

My tears welled in my eyes, and at that exact time, Anthony came out of the bathroom. My mother must have thought we were alone because her whole demeanor changed.

"Hey, son-in-law!" she said to my husband.

I looked at her and then back at Anthony. From the tightness of his face, I knew he heard our conversation. I had never told him that my mother treated me like this because I was embarrassed. Who wants to tell people their mother is verbally abusive?

Anthony's laughter was a sign that things were about to shift in the hallway. "Ain't no hey! Who the fuck you were talking to just now? I know not my fucking wife."

I turned and placed my hand on Anthony's chest, but when he looked down at me, I knew he was too far gone. His normally greenish, grey eyes were now a dark brownish black. That was never a good sign. His eyes changed with his mood.

"Son, what are you talking about?" My mother feigned ignorance but Anthony clearly wasn't having it.

"Yo, get the fuck out my house. Ain't no way you about to be around me, her, or our seed if that's how you feel."

Anthony moved me to the side and grabbed my mother's arm, not in a rough manner, but still aggressive, and moved her to the door. When we walked out in the living room, my father stood.

"Son, what's going on?" My father's face was etched in concern and confusion. I ran over to my father and hugged him. His kiss to my forehead had always been a calming force.

"I'll tell you this broad has to get out my house, talking reckless to my wife. I don't care if she feels a way about you having your girl here." Anthony was mad, and when he got like this, I stayed out of his way.

My father shook his head because he already knew she was on her stupid stuff again.

"Woman, can't you act right for once in your life? Our daughter is about to have your grandbaby and you can't even be a mother to her on today. The best thing you ever did was walk out the door on me."

My mother's face was turned the color of a tomato. We shared the same fair skin and I honestly looked a lot like my mother. She was a beautiful woman, but spitefulness, bitterness and age had not done her well.

"Nigga, fuck you and that bitch over there. I say what I say because I want better for her. If you had wanted something more for her maybe she wouldn't have been too fat to carry the first baby. Now she's going to..."

Anthony had yanked her with so much force to the door and pushed her out that she never got a chance to finish her sentence. Ava was now standing next to me and my dad. He had us both enclosed in his arms. I had tears running down my face and I was embarrassed in front of everyone. I hated the look of pity and for a second, I understood Ava not wanting people to know her status. Yes, this was a different situation and not as detrimental, but the shame I felt with this, I could only imagine hers. Anthony walked over to me with softened eyes and took me out of my father's hold.

Placing my face in his hands, he kissed my lips.

"You are perfect. You have always been perfect. Don't ever in your life let anyone, even me, make you feel like you're not." I placed my face in his chest and mumbled how embarrassed I was. "Don't be embarrassed, she should be. Now you gonna tell me what I'm having, or do I have to go bribe someone to tell me?"

He always knew how to make me smile. We moved the party to the back yard so we could finally do the gender reveal. Ava came up with the idea of confetti cannons and that was fine with me. She was pulling one and Isaac, who was the godfather, was pulling the other. We all counted to three, and when they pulled them, there was a popping noise then blue confetti went everywhere. Anthony actually started crying and it made me cry. I thanked God for allowing us another opportunity to be parents. We weren't out of the woods yet, but I had faith that God was going to give us a cup that overflowed for what we lost. We deserved it.

Looking around the yard after all the guests were gone, I wondered who the hell was going to clean up all this damn confetti. Ava's ass was in the house with Isaac, arguing, and they were getting on my not even my last nerve because Anthony was on that. They were on the remnants of a nerve that was forming. Watching Anthony coming my way with a big smile made all of this worth it.

"Hey, baby mama. Let's go lay down so I can talk to my boy."

I laughed at him calling me baby mama.

"Boy, who's going to clean this yard?"

His face screwed up in the ugliest of ways.

"Fuck you mean? The people who do our yard. I pay them enough. Come on, bae, I want to talk to my boy." His pout made me side-eye him as I got up from my seat. If my babe wanted to talk to his boy, then that's what we would do.

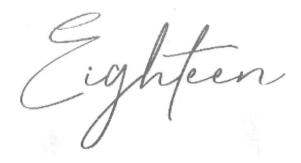

Ava

It had been the three longest weeks of my damn life
feels like. I blocked Isaac from all communications from me
and had to change my locks because his crazy ass came over
the next day after I told him to get out. I got home from
work to watch the sun set and this fool was sitting on my
patio with a glass of my wine, waiting on me. I wanted to slap
his ass. It took me an hour to get him out of my house. I
almost missed the damn sun setting. I was so excited about
Myah's gender reveal, though.

Only me and her knew the sex of the baby but Anthony's
ass had all but offered the baby up for me to tell him the
gender. When he offered the trip to the Maldives, I had to
take a step back because I had a moment of weakness. I was
about to tell it, but then I thought better of it since I was
supposed to be going to Jamaica soon anyway.

I hate to admit it, but I wore these short ass shorts to get
on Isaac's nerves. Even though I never gave dudes the time of

day, I would definitely let them look a bit. Myah's baby shower was lit; any time they had an event it was lit. I saw them duck off and I already knew what that was about.

I really never understood why Myah still even dealt with her mother because, and I say this with a lot of conviction, her mother was a bitch. She had always been a bitch to Myah since she was a kid. She never treated her bad in front of other people and that was why I was so surprised with her actions today. My uncle came with his new wife and I knew it was going to be a problem. Not many people knew that he was remarried but I was happy for him because he was genuinely happy. When Anthony threw her ass out, I was so damn happy. Well, that was until Isaac's ass snatched me up in a back room as I walked by.

"Ahhh! Isaac, what the hell are you doing?" He slammed the door behind him, and when he turned around, I giggled on the inside because the bull was raging.

"Ava, you got me fucked up around here with these damn shorts on. The fuck you on, ma?"

I stood in front of him with my arms across my chest and a stoic facial expression.

"Last I checked, we are not together, so why are you worried about what I have on?" I moved to pass him and sit on the bed. I wanted him to see just how much of my petty ass was hanging out.

Isaac laughed when I walked past him.

"Ava, you got me completely fucked up. I don't recall us breaking up. Just because your little mad ass put me out of your place after we had an argument, don't mean we fucking broke up. Grow the fuck up, ma."

Damn, now I was mad. "Me grow up? Boy, bye. You the one who said you wanted to be in this adult relationship. You know what, I don't have time for this shit. I have to prep the cannons."

I moved around him and walked out of the room as fast as I could. The nerve of his ass telling me I need to grow up. I know my situation is not easy, but I was still a woman and most of all a person. I wanted to be loved like any woman. My status is something I have to live with for the rest of my life, I didn't need a reminder of it. I take a pill just like he does now, every day. Him telling me I would be "waiting a while" was what took me over the top. It was as if he was saying, I should be grateful that he was with me. Well, I don't want to be with a man who is scared to have sex with me...HIV and all. I do *everything* I'm supposed to so I could achieve and keep my undetectable status. It may not seem like a lot to most, but to me, it was a big deal. I had only had sex with my late husband, and I wanted to try another one out at some point in my life.

I was so excited when the cannons shot out and Anthony's face was priceless. He picked Myah up in the biggest hug and when I saw the tears, I was in tears. The party had been long over and here was Isaac back in my face, talking trash.

"Ava, why you playing with me? You know I'm not going anywhere so stop with this little girl shit."

See, he was not about to keep calling me a little girl or insinuating I need to grow up.

I shifted on my feet in front of him before looking in his eyes. "If I'm such a little girl or need to grow up, leave me alone."

I tried to walk away but was pulled back into his chest. His lips on my neck made me weak. Damn, he knew that was my spot. The devil is busy.

"Ava, you feel that? That spark? That's how I know you mine. We're gonna work this shit out and when I come to your house tonight, you better unlock that damn door. I apologize for making you feel any kind of way because you know that's not what I ever mean to do. Be patient with me, bae; I promise it will be worth it." Him kissing my neck had me weak and I hated to admit that.

I could talk a lot of trash, but at the end of the day, I knew when he came by tonight, I was unlocking that door.

Being a man of his word, he came by around ten-thirty and I got my ass up and answered that door with haste. We didn't have sex, which annoyed me, but we held each other until we fell asleep. I wanted it to work with Isaac and I would give it my all to make sure it did from my end.

⚜

SINCE MYAH'S GENDER REVEAL, ISAAC AND I HAVE BEEN doing fine. I mean, it had only been two weeks, but we were trying to move forward. I was trying to be patient with the no sex, but we had graduated to digital sex – finger fucking, and we had used toys but that didn't make me feel much better. Tonight, we were having a double date, in-home dinner with Myah and Anthony. We were doing it at their home since they had a small movie theater and Myah and I were cooking.

The men were in the theater, playing the gaming system while we cooked. I absolutely loved to cook, and this would be my first time cooking for Isaac. I had cooked for Myah and Anthony tons of times but not since my status became known to him. I was hesitant this time, but Myah basically cursed me out about it.

"Girl, I see you got your mind right and forgave that man," Myah commented as she peeled potatoes. All I could do is shake my head.

"Man, he wasn't playing fair with the kisses on the neck." I laughed as I cut shrimp. Myah was laughing because I knew that was one of her spots too.

"Girl, these men folks don't be playing fair hardly ever."

I had to agree with her, especially fine men.

"What y'all in here yapping about?" Anthony walked in the kitchen and startled me. The knife slipped and I cut my finger.

"Shit!" I immediately grabbed my finger and moved to the sink. Myah came over to look if it was a bad cut. Isaac was not far behind.

Myah grabbed the first aid kit from the cabinet and began to get me fixed up. Hearing a noise, I turned around to see Anthony throwing the food away. Not just the shrimp but all the food, even the food I hadn't handled. Myah turned and her face said everything.

"Anthony, what are you doing? Why did you throw all of that away, boy?" She walked over to him.

He shifted on his feet and down casted his eyes at me. "Nah, it's cool, ma. We can go out."

That angered me because I knew why he wanted to go out. I walked over to the trash and looked inside to see that the knife I had cut myself with was also in there. They had a very expensive knife set that was gifted to them at their wedding. It was engraved.

"Wow!" That was really all I could say. Isaac walked over to me and kissed my forehead.

"It's cool, bae, we can just go out to eat."

That made matters worse because he didn't see the wrong in the situation. "So, because I lightly cut myself, we all of a sudden can go out to fucking eat. Is that it? No one wants to eat Positive shrimp?"

Myah moved to me, but I backed away from her and my tears started.

"You know what? I'm tired. I'm so fucking tired! I didn't ask for this shit! I didn't! Anthony, asshole! All you had to do was put the knife in the fucking dishwasher, furthermore half the shit you threw out your wife prepared. Since we throwing out shit I touched, let's do it."

I walked to the cabinet that held their plates and opened it. I had eaten off of all of them at some time or another. "Well, look what we have here. Ate off of all of these."

I took my hand and pulled the plates from the cabinet, not bothering to catch them before they hit the floor. I did the same with the glasses and silverware. I looked back and I could tell everyone as in shock.

"There! Now you can start fucking over. I got rid of it all! Let's throw everything Ava touches away right! Hell, while we at it, why not throw the whole bitch away? I got a nigga that won't fuck me and a best friend's husband who is like a brother but he will barely hug me!" I was in an irate state. I knew it because my head was starting to hurt.

Myah had tears in her eyes. "Ava, baby. Anthony didn't mean it like that."

"Bullshit, Mya! Bullshit! You know what, fuck everybody!"

I had to get out of there. I ran out of the kitchen and I could feel Isaac on my heels, but thank God for auto-start. I got in my car and was gone. I knew if I went home, they would follow, so I decided I would go to a hotel.

As I laid in my room at the Omni Hotel Uptown, I just knew I needed to get the hell away from all of this. Taking my phone out, I booked a plane ticket to Jamaica for the next morning. Fuck it, I was getting the hell out of here. I'll submit emergency leave papers in the morning after I pop in my crib to pack a bag and get my laptop. I needed time to just be with me. I felt like I was losing myself in others' thoughts of me and I promised I would never do that. It was time to turn an Ava's Day into an Ava's month.

I HAD BEEN IN JAMAICA FOR TWO WEEKS NOW AT AN amazing Sandals Resort that had over-the-water bungalows. When I went home the morning after the Armageddon of dinners at Myah's house before my flight, I packed about two to three weeks of clothes and my laptops. While I was at the airport, I submitted for an emergency mental health leave and my doctor submitted the corresponding paperwork. I decided I was going to throw caution to the wind and stay for a full month. The staff at the resort was amazing and I loved them, from my cleaning ladies to the room service staff. My bungalow was gorgeous, and it had a hammock that I had slept in at least five times since I'd been here.

I knew that me just disappearing would worry Myah and I didn't want her to have any complications, so I FaceTimed her. I didn't tell her where I was because I didn't want her to pop up. I hadn't talked to Isaac at all and he had called, attempted to FaceTime and left numerous text messages. They ranged from apologies to threats if I didn't call "my man" back. It was extremely entertaining, to say the least. My travel agent was able to lock me into an amazing deal since I was staying so long, and I was grateful. For the past two weeks, I had literally worn nothing but bathing suits and it felt awesome. I went shopping to make sure I had enough clothes to last me, but my cleaning lady took my laundry every three days and comes back the next day with them washed. By the time I leave here, I would have tipped her well over a thousand dollars.

Today, I decided to go on a date with my-damn-self and I brought the most beautiful dress. I had set up a sexy ass dinner on the beach with my favorite meal plan: seafood! My dress was a black and pink bodycon dress that had the entire back out. You could see the dimples in my lower back, and I didn't give a damn. Since I was on the beach, I opted for no shoes because I wanted to feel the sand between my toes. Of course, I scheduled my dinner so that I would be sitting on the beach during the sunset because it was the best view. As I was escorted to my table, I admired the beauty around me. For a split second, I wondered if I could find a job here, but then reality set in. My doctor was the leading doctor in HIV and AIDS treatment and research, so it would not be smart for me to move treatment. I hated that I felt tied to a life that I may not necessarily want to live. My medication was expensive and even though I was extremely financially stable, that could change quick if I ever lost my amazing health coverage that I had. I am tied to a corporate job that, although I am good at what I do, I don't love it. I love the beach, I love painting, and honestly...I was pretty good at it. It was one of my guilty pleasures that even Myah didn't know about. I did have my art hung in my condo, but I painted under a brush name.

Sitting at my table on the beach as I drank my Jamaican punch, my mind drifted to Isaac. I missed him so much, but I was tired. I was tired of being in some pseudo-relationship with a man who was not able to fully be with me because of fear. He knew exactly what he was getting himself into. I didn't ask him to want to be with me. I shouldn't feel lonely in a relationship. God knows I appreciated his effort, but at the end of the day, regardless of how this might sound, it wasn't enough. The sun setting brought me out of my thoughts, and I smiled at how beautiful it looked over the water.

"That sunset is beautiful, but it definitely doesn't compare to your beauty." Looking down at my cup, I realized I must have had one too many of these punches because I was starting to hear things. Isaac's voice sounded so clear. Wow.

Feeling a presence on my left, I turned to see Isaac standing there in a white wife beater, linen shorts that showed his dick print clearly, and no shoes. His dreads were loose, and he looked sexy as fuck. I had to look down at my cup again because now I was hallucinating. Damn, I can't drink any more of these things.

"Damn, I'm straight tripping."

I laughed at myself as I got up. I stumbled a bit and that confirmed to me that I had definitely drank too much. I walked towards the hallucination only to walk into a hard chest and fall flat on my ass. I looked up, quickly realizing he was really here.

What the fuck!

Nineteen

I saac

BEING WITH AVA WAS THE BIGGEST DAMN CHALLENGE I had ever had to endure. I knew I loved her, although I had yet to tell her. We were good as hell after we made up the night of Myah's gender reveal. I was working on getting past my own thoughts on the sex thing and it was coming closer and closer to the time. We hadn't fucked yet, or even me doing oral, although I had tasted her on my fingers. She tasted good as hell. A part of me ignorantly thought she would have a weird taste or something. I feel bad as hell thinking that way, but hell, I didn't know. I'd never been in this situation. My uncle and auntie had become my sounding board and voice of reason. I wanted to love this girl the way she needed to loved. It was all going good 'til that damn dinner. I wasn't really thinking when I agreed with Anthony that we could just go out to eat.

When she blew up, I couldn't lie and say I understood. I didn't understand why she reacted that way until I spoke with my auntie. She made me have an understanding of the feeling of worthlessness. My auntie cooks for my uncle and their children all the time. She said the same thing Ava did: all he had to do was put the knife in the dishwasher. Ava would more than likely had thrown the shrimp away not because she has HIV but because no one would want to cook food that had blood on it, period.

When Ava left, I thought she was going to get her head together and I would just stop by the next day around sunset to talk to her. When she didn't answer at first, I wasn't tripping, but on day three, I was mad as hell. I went to Myah and Anthony's, ready for war if she didn't tell me something. She said she didn't know and that pissed me off more, but when Ava's little ass called her on FaceTime and I saw her ass was on a beach somewhere, I was about to lose it. Anthony had to pull me out of the room before I talked and let her know I was there. She had me all the way fucked up if she thought disappearing on me was cool. I don't give a damn what we go through, as a grown ass man and woman, we should be able to work through it. I knew exactly what I signed up for. Never once since I started taking them have I stopped taking my PrEP pills. Ava was going to learn how to put some respect on my damn effort. Talking to my auntie, she told me to give her time, but when we got into week two, time was fucking up.

After finally convincing Myah, she gave me the spare key to Ava's condo and I went on my search. I looked all up and through her shit with no damn remorse. Sitting at her desk, I looked around it in frustration. I just wanted to find out where the fuck my girl went so I could fix this. Moving papers she had beside her laptop, I saw a business card from a travel agent. I didn't waste any time calling the number. It took a lot of smooth talking, but she finally told me where my baby was and I booked a damn flight. I booked the flight for three days away so I could get a game plan and know exactly what I really wanted to do. Me taking this flight was in my mind me saying I was all into this relationship and I knew what I had to do to be all in. Honestly, I was more than ready after the talks with my uncle and auntie. I was ready to be with Ava, one hundred percent.

❧

LOOKING DOWN AT AVA IN THIS TIGHT ASS DRESS, I HAD TO shake my head. Her little ass was drunk and that was evident by her conversation with her cup. I had to laugh as I leaned down to help her up. I pulled her into my arms as soon as she got her balance. It had been too long since I had her in my arms. I felt her relax in my arms then as if she realized what she was doing, her body tensed up. She pulled away from me and still had a look as if she couldn't believe I was here.

"Isaac, how did you... what are you doing here?" I was stuck on her beauty and this little ass dress, with no back.

"You thought I wasn't gonna come looking for your fine ass, Ava? You mine and you running every time some shit goes down is not going to work. I know the only man you are used to is Andre, but I mean this with every ounce of respect in me: he's gone, I'm here. I want to love you because I do love you."

Her eyes bugged then welled with tears.

She shifted on her feet. "You love me?"

I answered her question with a kiss to her lips. "Yes, I love you."

Her first tear released. "You love me even though..."

I had to stop her from talking because I already knew what it was. "No, I don't love you even though, I love you just because."

The rest of her tears caught up in the race with her first

tear and I kissed them away. The sun had already set so we were just standing there on the beach on some Harlequin romance shit. We eventually made it back to her bungalow. For the rest of the night, we talked about everything from us to Myah and Anthony's son. She confirmed that I was still taking my pill a day and I was. I had actually got tested a few days prior to coming here. I wanted to get everything that we needed to talk about off of our chest. I wanted her mind and heart clear so that we could move forward because I had plans for her tomorrow, and I didn't need any doubt in the way.

We ended up falling asleep on the overwater hammock on the bungalow's patio. Waking up with her in my arms was everything I wanted and more of what I needed. I had a full day planned for my babe and it all started with the knock on the door, which was the breakfast I ordered. Because I knew Ava could eat her ass off, I made sure she had a variety of food, and she partook in all of the variety. After breakfast, I told my babe to take a shower because she had a full spa day. I had everything taken care of even her dress for dinner tonight, which was already at the spa. Myah helped me plan this too because I liked doing this kind of stuff for my girl, but I didn't know anything about planning it. When they came to pick her up for her day, she was surprised as hell. I needed every minute she was gone to get everything in place.

Hours later, I was waiting for my queen at Eleanor's, one of the restaurants on the South Coast Sandals resort. The dress I picked out for her was a peplum style black dress with a pair of pink heels. My baby loves pink. She was gorgeous coming in with her hair in its natural state. I loved her hair like this. I have to admit, I love it short. Watching her walk towards me made my heart smile just as much as her smile showed on her face. It was reaching her eyes and that made me feel like the man. She immediately came where she belonged: my arms.

I kissed her forehead then looked in the eyes of the woman I knew I would love forever. "You look beautiful."

I know we were in public, but I had to grab her ass. She told me a while ago that if I didn't grab her ass when I kiss her then I didn't love her. I had to laugh at her when she said that because one had nothing to do with the other, but hey, if that's how she feels, I'll govern myself according. Pulling her seat out for her, she sat down after I kissed her neck. I knew that was her spot, so I had a plan to touch every spot she had tonight.

"How was your day?" The way her face lit up, I knew it was worth every expensive ass penny.

"Oh my God, babe! It was amazing! Thank you so much! Those people at the spa made me feel like a queen. My body feels so refreshed. They kept calling me Mrs. Mills, though." Just as she said that they brought out our salads.

We prepped our salads to eat and once she took her first bite, I decided to respond to her statement. "Good, they follow instructions."

I gave the strict instruction to refer to her as Mrs. Mills. I just wanted her to try it on and from the redness in her cheeks I think it fit well. Our main dishes were amazing and, of course, my babe ate off my plate like she always does. Greedy little ass. I told her ass no dessert, though, and her ass actually pouted. I had something real special for dessert. I had planned the dinner so that it ended at least an hour and a half before the sun set because I wanted to watch the sun set from our bungalow. The restaurant wasn't far from the bungalow, so we walked back in no time. Once we got to the door, I wrapped my arms around her, pulling her into my chest.

Kissing her on her neck then moving to her ear, I declared, "I love you."

I didn't need a response to my declaration, so I unlocked the door and pushed it open. The sound of her gasp made me smile. Pink and white rose petals trailed the floor out to the patio. There were candles everywhere and I was extremely pleased with myself.

Ava turned in my arms to face me. "You... you did this for me?"

I wasn't sure why there was doubt in her voice. She was the only one in the room with me, so who else would this be for? "Yes, babe, this is all for you."

Her tears showed her appreciation and my kiss showed my appreciation for hers. We hadn't made it to the patio, but I wanted to get there because I had less than forty-five minutes before the sun began to set. Moving her to the patio, our shoes were already off as we walked on the beach to get here. I was wearing a linen short set, which was easy to peel off if needed. As we walked to the patio, I unzipped her dress. She grabbed the front.

"Isaac, I don't have on a bra. Are we going on the patio?" I had to laugh at the fear in her eyes when she turned around. Lil Babe was scared but she didn't need to be.

"Yeah, we are." I moved to whisper in her ear as if we were in a room full of people although we were alone. "You don't want to be daddy's freak?"

The smirk on her face told me she just might be. Without my help, Ava slipped out of her dress letting it fall to the floor. Damn, all that's mine and I'm about to show her just how much. After taking my shirt off, I kissed Ava with the same passion of the love I have for her. I move us towards the patio where I had a cushioned pallet set out for us. Before stepping past the threshold of the patio, I picked up the remote to the sound system to turn it on.

"In the thunder and rain

You stare into my eyes
I can feel your hand
Movin' up my thighs
Skirt around my waist
Wall against my face
I can feel your lips
Oooh
I don't wanna stop just because
People walkin' by are watchin' us
I don't give a damn what they think
I want you now
I don't wanna stop just because
You feel so good inside of my love
I'm not gonna stop no no no
I want you
All I wanna say is
Any time
And any place
I don't care who's around
Any time
And any place
I don't care who's around
Nonononono
Weeoooh-hooo
Oooooooohooo
Hoohoo"

This, tonight, was about my babe and her pleasure and satisfaction. We stood at the edge of the pallet with her in nothing but a thong and me just in boxer briefs. I stopped kissing her to look into her eyes because I wanted her to realize what was about to happen. There was no fucking going back from this point. She looked at me with questionable eyes and I wanted to answer her unspoken question.

"Can I have you, Ava?" I wanted to hear her tell me that I could have her. I mentally knew that but in this delicate situation, it was an important part of this process.

"Yes, you can have me. Can I have you?"

I gave her a smirk. "You already have me."

She looked out at the ocean as if she was in thought. Finally, she turned her attention back to me. "I won't be offended if you use a condom."

I smiled because my uncle told me, a sign of her love would be to protect me. Even though we had all of the components to the safety formula, she still wanted to add an extra level of protection. I appreciated her for that. I wanted her to feel comfortable, so I stepped back into the bungalow and grabbed the condoms that I already had on the table. Walking back out, I stopped in my tracks as I watched the beauty before me.

Ava was laying on the pallet with her legs wide and fingers playing in Heaven's gates. I watched her for a beat, then I kneeled before her. Her moans drew me in, and I was stuck. Moving her fingers, I replaced it with my tongue. She tasted good.

"Ah, Isaac! It feels so good!" I was focused on her clit and pulling as much pleasure out of her from it. She was trying to run from my tongue, so I had to hold her little ass in place. While I was partaking in my dessert, I slid the condom on. Coming up for air, my timing was perfect as I saw the sun beginning to set. Kissing up her middle, feeling her hands in my dreads made my dick harder. When I reached her neck, I made sure to leave my mark. The music had long ago changed and now it was playing some throwback Fantasia.

"I been thinking 'bout this
All day long
Can't believe how I'm gone

And my minds blown off of you
I'm anticipating(oh)
When you're coming home(oh)
See tonight we're 'bout to try out something new
I was thinking role play if you're ready, boy get ready
(Let's see you be Denzel)
It's your training day boy come and get me, are you with me
Let's keep the lights on cause tonight I wanna watch you
perform
(Let me see what cha got for yo girl now baby)
When I turn you on you steal the show boy you should get an
award
(As a matter a fact boy ya know that I do)
I nominate you
Can't no other brother put that thing down like you do
Ain't no other way to say it baby you're the truth
Keep doing what you do
I'm nominating you
I nominate you
For the best kissing and love scene
For the best sequel that I've seen
You know what I mean boy you're the truth
Keep doing what you do
I'm nominating you"

Just as the sun set, I slid into the woman I love. Well, it wasn't really a slide, it was more like a squeeze. The memory hit me that she hasn't had sex in over five years. Her walls fit tight around my thick nine inches. Damn, she felt good as fuck. I can't believe I waited this fucking long to feel her walls. I moved with excellence as I allowed her wetness to guide the way. Her back was arched, and her nails were digging in my back.

"Isaac, babe. You feel so good. I love you."

I intensified my strokes to show my love for her, but I still made sure to tell her with my words. The moon reflecting off the water combined with the music and subtle sound of the waves was a beautiful track to our lovemaking but now, I was ready to fuck.

After kissing the lobe of her ear, I said what I had been waiting to say. "Someone told me you wanted to be fucked. Let ya man fuck you." I slid out of her slowly. "Turn that ass over and make sure you get my arch right, Ava. Daddy likes it deep."

Ava flipped her ass over so damn fast, I thought she was going to fall. I chuckled a bit, but when she dipped that back, I ain't have shit to laugh about. Arch was perfect. Yeah, this Daddy's! I slid back in with force and hit the bottom.

"Isaac! Oh, God!"

Yeah, I was tearing that ass up. Ava has dimples in her lower back that served as grips for me and I was loving that shit.

"You mine, ma. This mine. I love your ass." I felt my nut rising and I was finally going to have my one to her three or more now.

When that nut hit me, it made a nigga weak as fuck. I stayed in her for a beat longer, then pulled out, causing her to fall forward. Her hair was all over her head from putting it in the pillow cushion of the pallet. I laid beside her and pulled her in my arms. We both were still breathing hard as hell. Damn. Bae pussy so good, it put me to sleep because the next thing I remember is waking up to her removing my condom and cleaning me off. I looked at my watch and it was almost ten at night.

"Damn, pussy putting a nigga to sleep."

She laughed as she cleaned me with a warm washcloth.

"I didn't think you would want to sleep out here with a wet dick."

I chuckled and got up after she finished. She had put on some clothes, well not really. She had on my wife beater, but from the jiggle in her ass I could tell no panties.

I followed her in the bungalow and let her know I was jumping in the shower then I'd come to bed. As I stood under the water of the shower, I thought about the night. I didn't have any regrets because the night was perfect. The woman I loved and who loved me is HIV positive and that didn't negate any of the feelings I felt for her. She took care of herself and made sure I did the same. Even tonight with her mentioning the condom, she was still taking care of me. Before I came here to get her runaway ass, I asked Dr. Thomas if I had to use a condom and he told me I didn't. Again, with her undetectable status and low viral load there was a ninety-two to ninety-six percent chance that she would not pass it to me. If you add on top of that me taking my Truvada faithfully, I really had no worries. I used the condom because I wanted her to feel comfortable about this decision we were making.

Getting out the shower, I wrapped my towel around my waist and stepped out of the bathroom after brushing my teeth. When I came into the bedroom Ava was in the bed, already asleep. I stood there and just looked at her as she laid with the cover over one leg and the other sticking out. She was on her side and my wife beater had risen to show he nude plump ass. Damn. I walked over to the dresser where some of my stuff was set and pulled out my pill bottle. I opened the bottle while I still watched her. She was so gorgeous, and she was mine, HIV and all. After popping the pill in my mouth, I walked to the bed and pulled my towel off. Daddy wanted some more of her, so I was about to wake her back up with these strokes.

A nthony

TONIGHT, WE HAD A FAMILY DINNER AT MAMA LILLI AND
Pop Solomon's house. They were going to be meeting Ava for
the first time. Isaac was nervous as hell and I was laughing at
his ass, hard. I remember introducing them to Myah. I was
sweating bullets and praying they liked her and they loved
her. Sometimes I wonder if they are more loyal to her than
me based on how they act when she comes crying to them
about something. At thirty-one weeks pregnant now, there
was always something that annoyed her thick ass.

"Myah, babe. Are you almost ready?" I had been in my
mancave for an hour and a half waiting on Myah to get
dressed. I was ready to go so we could eat. Myah not
answering me caused me to turn my game off and go see
about her.

I called her name as I walked to the back of our house
and when I got to our bedroom, I had to take a damn picture

for the Gram. My baby was laid back on the bed with one shoe halfway on and the other in her hand, sleeping. She was fully clothed, but my son had her belly so big she couldn't get her shoes on. I loved the fuck out of her ass. I went over and took the shoe out of her hand, waking her up. She tried to sit up, but I had to help her.

"Babe, I was coming. I was just resting my eyes." I kissed her lips because her ass got out of the shower over two hours ago. We showered together because she wanted some shower dick. I never have a problem serving her dick wherever she wants it.

"I know, baby, I just want to help you get ya shoes on." I finally took notice of the shoes she was putting on and my face screwed up. "My, I already told you about these damn heels."

My's pout was cute as hell but I wasn't about to play with her. "Babe, it's only three inches and it's blocked. That doesn't even count as a heel."

I didn't even say anything as I put her heel on because it would have been a waste of time. When she stood up and I pressed her against me, I felt my son kick against her stomach. I smiled because he had a strong ass kick. He shows his ass when I'm in my pussy and I pop the fuck out of her belly. He won't be a blocker from the womb on my watch. Pregnancy fit my wife and after our boy turns maybe two-years-old I wanted another one. I need a little girl that looks just like her. I kissed her lips before ushering her out of the room so we could leave. I was ready to eat, and Mama messed up and told me she made a lemon pound cake. Yeah, we needed to get there.

EVERYBODY WAS ALREADY AT THE HOUSE WHEN WE GOT there, including Unc' Mase and Aunt Marci. I loved them and just like Mama and Pops took me in as family so did they. Food could immediately be smelled when you stepped into the house and my stomach sounded off. I looked at My who looked as hungry as I did. When she looked at me, I couldn't help but wink at her sexy ass.

"Is that my other babies?" Hearing my Mama as we walked deeper into the house, I had to smile. Ever since I've been in her life, she has loved me like I came from her womb and Pops from his nut sack.

Walking in the family room, Isaac was sitting on the over-sized lounge chair with Ava basically on his lap. My bro looked genuinely happy and I was eternally grateful to Ava for allowing him to find peace in her. My Unc and Aunt were in the corner hugged up like they were in a club or something. They had literally been like that since I've known them. I'm surprised they don't have more kids. Mama came over and hugged me and Myah. She was so excited to become a grand-mother and I'm happy I could make that happen for her. Isaac got up from his seat to greet me. I haven't seen him since he's been back from his trip with Ava and that was over a month ago.

Taking me into a bro hug, we greeted each other.

"Bruh, it's good seeing you." I missed him and we defi-nitely needed to get up.

"I know, man. Been busy as hell with the new contract and keeping that smile on my babe's face." Looking over at Ava, her smile was bigger than I had ever seen. I wanted to make things right with her and before I leave it will be done.

"I feel you, man, you know I stay on the job with My. My boy got her clingy but I love that." We laughed together until Mama came in and told us dinner was ready.

Mama loved entertaining so she had a formal dining room

that set twenty damn people. The table was custom built and expandable. We all sat coupled up and I was honestly surprised not to see Unc and Aunt's kids. I guess this was an adult dinner. The women were bringing in the food. Mama showed the hell out! Fried and baked chicken, fried pork chops, roast, green beans, collard greens, corn, rice, mashed potatoes, baked macaroni and cheese, and candied yams. I already knew me and bae was more than likely going to be taking one of the guest rooms here tonight. We said grace and started eating. Multiple conversations were going on at one time until Unc asked Ava and Isaac how everything was going.

Ava looked to Isaac as if asking him to answer. "We doing good, Unc. I'm happy I followed my heart like you did."

That statement made me arch my eyebrow because I felt like there was an underlying meaning. I guess I was about to find out exactly what it meant. I promise you learn new things about people every day regardless of how long you have known them.

My Aunt put her fork down and wiped her mouth. "I see you looking crazy over there, nephew. I don't think you know this about me but I'm HIV positive. Have been for over fourteen years. Two years before I meant Mase I was brutally gang-raped and from that I was infected with HIV When I met your Uncle, I pushed him away but he was overly persistent. Clearly, there came a time that I had to tell him about my HIV and I need you to understand, that the research and treatment available today was not there back then. It was not cool or accepted to be with someone with this virus. I was ashamed and just like I thought, Mase ran the other way.

We would see each other out and he actually dated another woman. He would talk to me and we \ became good friends. Well, because I'm amazing, he couldn't resist and our story began. It wasn't easy on this journey, but we are here with four beautiful children. I have been undetectable for a very long time."

I felt like the room wasn't moving. I was at a loss for words, like damn. I never knew and the way Unc loved Aunt, I would never think any of this. I looked at Ava and she had tears in her eyes. Isaac wrapped his arm around her, pulling her in for a forehead kiss. I'm not sure if this was her first time hearing it, but I could tell it wasn't Isaac's.

Ava shifted in her seat. "I didn't know you were positive. Can I talk to you sometimes?"

Aunt Marci smiled at Ava genuinely. "Baby, you're a part of the family now. You can come see and talk to me anytime. Come without Isaac so we can girl talk."

We all laughed. I felt like I needed to say something, but I wasn't sure what. I did know I needed to apologize.

"Ava, I wanted to apologize for tripping at dinner awhile back. I have to be real with you. Ever since I found out about your status, I've blamed you for something that maybe I shouldn't have."

Her face scrunched up and head tilted to the side. "Blamed me for what?

I looked at Myah because this was information she didn't know. She had a confused look on her face, and I knew what I was about to say might upset her but if I was going to get it off my chest, all of it had to go. "I blamed you for My losing my son."

Myah jumped up from her seat and I grabbed her hand to stop her from moving or slapping me. I knew she was upset because I saw the tears, so I placed my hand on her stomach. She looked down at my hand and without me even having to give instruction she sat down. Although she was upset, I still pulled her in to kiss her lips. Her tears were falling, and I told her I loved her against her lips. I turned my attention back to Ava and she had tears falling as well. Isaac looked like he wanted to fight me, but I wanted to leave here clear in my heart.

"Ava, the last time My was pregnant, it was after Andre died. Clearly, I didn't know about your status but after that time Myah was with you more than me. Hell, I don't even know when we had the time to get pregnant. For a long time, I blamed My and that's why I initially didn't want another baby. When I found out about your status, I shifted the blame to you. I was mad and being real, I really didn't have a reason to be. I was hurt and I apologize as a man for treating you a way, sis. I need you to know, I don't have a problem with your status. I love you, Ava, and I'm so happy my brother found you."

Ava's tears were flowing, and I felt bad. "I didn't know you felt that way. I...I never meant to hurt Myah. I didn't know. I was so lost then, and I admit, I was selfish. I monopolized her time because of my grief. Myah, I'm so sorry."

Myah stood from her seat and walked over to Ava, causing her to stand. They embraced each other tightly before My pulled back to speak.

"Ava, you did absolutely nothing wrong. It was not your fault. I don't know why my son couldn't be here with us, but I know God has a plan."

I stood from the table and walked over to give my Lil' Sis a hug that I knew we both needed. She fell apart in my arms and I felt like a horrible brother because this was the first hug she had gotten from me since I found out about her status. Ava is one of the strongest women I know, and I thought that prior to even knowing about her status. Finding out about her status just amplified that strength. I was proud of all the women in this room currently. All of them had tears in their eyes, soft asses.

"Boy, you better had apologized or it was going to be problems." Mama stood up and came over to all of us and tried to group hug us with her little arms. Isaac stood to get some of mama's love, he's always been a jealous nigga. I love every person in this room more than they will ever know. When I didn't have a family, they took me in. When I didn't know love, Myah gave it to me freely until I was able to give it back correctly.

Twenty One

M yah

AVA BETTER COME ON SO I CAN GET THESE DAMN APPLE donuts. There is this amazing place in York, South Carolina called Windy Hill Orchard & Cidery and they have these cinnamon apple donuts that make you want to fight air they're so good. They are like cake donuts, but they are so soft and they serve them hot. Ever since I found out about them, I have been whining and making Anthony go get them or Ava but today, I want to pick apples! Ava is not pleased but I don't care, it's about me. I'm the Baby Mama.

"Myah! It's too hot to be picking apples! Why can't we just get the damn donuts and keep it moving?" Ava has been complaining since we got out here and that was only like ten minutes ago.

Hell, we're still standing in the line to buy the bags to go in the orchard. I guess she's annoyed because I had her go ahead and grab me a six-pack of donuts to eat while I'm in line waiting.

"Ava! Stop fussing. I'm gonna have you back to Isaac before you can blink sprung girl. Damn, finally get new dick and you don't know how to act, I swear."

Since she's returned from her little vacation turned baecation she's had a new waddle to her walk. Isaac must have put that thang on her, and I couldn't be happier for her. I could tell she was so in love and I wanted that for her more than anything. Right now, for me, all I wanted was to pick some apples and eat some cinnamon apple donuts. We finally got to the front of the line and got our bags to go in. I was so excited because they gave me an apple picker. It's this long stick that has prongs and a little basket on the end. I love gadgets.

"So, what's up with you and Isaac?" I asked the question as if I didn't already know because I'm nosey and love hearing about her newfound love.

Ava stopped in her tracks and I looked at her while shielding my eyes from the sun. It was hot as hell out here, but I wanted these apples. I didn't tell Anthony that I was coming out here because I knew he would have a fit. At thirty-four weeks now, I had surpassed how long I was pregnant with my son before I lost him, but Anthony was still on edge and I just wanted to be free. I wasn't an invalid. I was having so much fun picking these apples and Ava was just following behind me with the bags for me to drop them in.

We talked about her and Isaac as she tried to downplay how sprung she was. If that man calls, she goes running but I can't talk because I'm the same way. I'm just happy she finally has someone to run to. I had filled one bag and was on the way to fill the other. There was an apple that looked perfect and I wanted it! I had to literally go inside of the tree branches to reach it and it was still a bit of a reach. When I reached forward, a shooting pain shot through my back causing me to drop the apple picker and shout in pain.

"Myah! What's wrong?" Ava ran to me, fighting the branches to get out of her way.

I slowly backed up and took deep breaths calming myself down. "Nothing, nothing. I think I just stretched too far. I'm OK."

Ava looked worried as if she didn't believe me and being honest, I didn't believe myself, but I was not going to panic and cause more dismay. I did know one thing; I was ready to go now. We gathered our things and brought my donuts. Ava drove because I hated driving pregnant so she took me home and tucked me in the bed... with my donuts. I should feel ashamed that I brought two dozen, but I don't. I feel even less ashamed about eating a whole dozen before preparing to sleep.

This sleep was about to be good as hell too. Anthony was with Isaac having their little man day and I was pleased his ass wasn't annoying the hell out of me. I knew he was lurking though because he had Mason from Lourie's Security firm come all the way to Charlotte to install these cameras in our house. I wanted to curse him out knowing that man's wife was pregnant with triplets! She is the cutest little thing too. Mason's family and mine have a business relationship/friendship because his firm supplies all the security for our laundry mats and cleaners. I met his wife, Claire, when they were here a few months ago and I invited them to dinner. I thought I loved my man, but that girl is like a garment on Mason and I can't be mad. He is fine as hell.

I blew a kiss at the camera in the corner of our room then laid on my side. Not even one minute later my phone alerted me to a text and I knew it was from my husband because of the alert notification tone.

I love you too Fat Mama. Get some rest I'll be home soon.

His lurking ass. Sleep didn't take long to find me. This

cinnamon apple donut induced coma was about to be life until my baby got home.

༄

WAKING UP IN UNBEARABLE PAIN WAS NOT THE WAY I envisioned waking up. Anthony's head between my legs, yeah, but this hell no. I immediately grabbed my belly and felt my son kick which caused more pain. I sat up slowly to see if the pain would subside, but it didn't. I wasn't sure if Anthony was home yet so I waved my hand to the camera because if he was watching he would see me. I was moaning and trying to breathe through the pain.

I decided to grab some water in case I needed to hydrate. Moving out of my room towards the kitchen, I was finally scared. It was too early. As I got closer to the kitchen, I heard what sounded like him, Isaac, and a couple of other voices coming from his mancave which was right off the kitchen. Moving that way, a pain hit then I felt wetness on my inner thigh that caused me to lean on a small table that had some cups from last night. My quick hand movement made them crash to the floor and I went with them.

"What the fuck? Myah! Babe!" Hearing the fear in Anthony's voice scared me even more. I heard a lot of movement and knew the men were coming out of the room. Feeling Anthony's hands on my back my body wanted to relax but the pain was too much.

"Anthony, I think my water broke." Looking up at him with tears in my eyes, I labored my next statement. "It's too early."

I knew he was scared but he would never show me that. He helped me off the floor as the men sprang into action getting me into Anthony's truck. Isaac drove as Anthony was in the backseat with me as I cried through contractions and he helped me with breathing exercises. Now we had yet to take a class but I'm almost positive he was imitating whatever he may have seen on television. I didn't care in the moment, I just loved him for it. I could hear Isaac on the phone with who I could only assume was Ava. I'm sure she wants to kick my ass but whatever. It didn't take us long to get to the hospital and I was immediately rushed to a room. When they told me that my water had in fact broken and we were having a baby tonight, I immediately broke down.

"It's all my fault. Fucking apples!" I cried hard and Anthony was trying to console and calm me down.

"Myah, babe. Calm down. This is not your fault. Lil' man just wanted to come earlier." Anthony was kissing over my face. I just prayed that everything was going to be alright. I couldn't bear to lose another baby. It would kill me and probably my marriage. I should have just got the damn apple donuts like Ava said and kept it moving but no! I had to pick damn apples.

It didn't take long for Ava to get there and I could tell she was a little upset, but I knew she would never vocally say so. Everything happened so fast because I wasn't even able to get an epidural before I was told it was time to push. With my husband on one side of me and my best friend on the other, I pushed out my son, Maximus Anthony Montgomery.

My boy was only three pounds, four ounces but he was crying still. Not a loud cry but it was a cry I prayed to hear. Anthony was crying with him as he stood over the nurses as they cleaned him off and did what they needed to do. The nurse told me once he was clean, I could hold him quickly before they took him to the neonatal unit. It felt like forever but when they laid my son on my chest, everything in the world seemed right. Feeling Anthony's lips on my forehead, I looked up at him.

"You did good, My. I'm so proud of you." I smiled at his

statement and looked down at my beautiful son with a skin complexion to match ours.

Right as the nurse told me it was time for me to let him go, I kissed his little head and told him I loved him. When he opened his eyes slightly and I saw the greenish, grey eyes the world stopped. I looked at Anthony with teary eyes and a smile. "He has your eyes."

༺✦༻

It has been the longest five weeks ever. I was released from the hospital a week after Maximus was born and it was not without a fight. I was there every day for hours and so was Anthony. My breast milk had come in so I was pumping multiple times a day and storing it for the time that I could give it to him. Well, I kind of was because they were feeding it to him, but I was producing more than what he was eating. Ava and Isaac had visited their godson multiple times and were in love with him. I was so in love with my son, he was everything right in my life.

Sitting in the rocking chair holding him, I was so happy he was not hooked up to all those machines anymore. He was finally a little over five pounds and that was a great sign. The nurse even said she wouldn't be surprised if we could take him home soon. I was holding on to that hope like a crackhead holds a rock. He was a mixture of me and his father but had his father's eyes which I knew would be a problem with fast ass girls when he gets older.

"Mrs. Montgomery, would you like to feed him now?" I nodded my head to the nurse's question and reached my hand out to receive the bottle. She just smiled brightly at me. "No, I mean would you like to breastfeed him now?"

I looked at her with questionable eyes because I had yet

to breastfeed. I wanted to so bad and felt like I was being slighted because I couldn't. "I...I can breastfeed him now?"

The nurse, Emma, smiled before answering me. "You sure can. The doctor signed off on it this morning."

"But I don't know how." I was nervous. I mean I read the books and watched the videos but still didn't know what I was doing.

Emma ensured me that she would help. Emma took us to a private room and helped me position him. I found the football hold to be most comfortable. It took Max a few tries but when he latched on, I showed my happiness with tears. Hearing a clicking noise I looked up to see Anthony taking a picture of the moment and smiling. The love that was in his eyes I can honestly say I have never seen before. That was not a bad thing, my son had amplified his love level and I loved both of my boys. Anthony walked over and kissed my lips.

"You and my son are so perfect, and I thank God for you." Seeing the moisture rim his eyes made mine water.

It was all worth it. I almost lost myself when I lost my first son, but God saw fit to bless us with the most perfect son. He was beautiful and I wouldn't change a thing about what I've been through. In every life event, there is a lesson. Losing my son taught me to not take *anything* for granted and to take care of me first. If I was being honest about it all, my first pregnancy I was not thinking about my health or my son's, it was all about Ava. I don't blame her for this at all because I made that decision even when she shunned me. This pregnancy, she didn't allow me to even take care of her in any way. This time she made it all about me. I appreciated her for that because it was in my nature to try and take care of her.

My son is a reflection of me and his father's love for each

other. I'm so happy I went with my heart and agreed to have a baby because the amount of love I feel now I don't think I ever would have without Maximus.

Twenty Two

Ava

THESE LAST SIX MONTHS HAVE BEEN AMAZING, FROM THE birth of my godson to the love between me and Isaac. We of course had our issues like any other couple, but we persevered through them. I was still adhering to my ART therapy and he was adhering to his PrEP regimen. Every three months our doctor gave him an HIV test which of course was always negative. My viral load remained below the necessary threshold, continuously making me undetectable. I had been spending a lot of time with Auntie Marci, as she asked me to call her. I loved her so much because she had a full understanding of what I was feeling. I love Myah but the reality is, you just never truly know how this feels until you are living with it.

Isaac spent the majority of his time at my place and we were talking about moving in together, but I was hesitant because we really haven't been together that long. He clearly didn't care because slowly but surely my massive walk-in closet was becoming a his and hers. It started with a, "Bae pick my dry cleaning up and just put it in the closet." After about two of those a week, plus him bringing over a new bag of clothes almost every day, he now had a complete section in my closet. I loved everything about being in a relationship with Isaac. He went out of his way to make me feel loved every day. I don't know how I went so long without having someone to love me the way he does. We rarely talk about my status, because it was unnecessary. We had long ago gone over the risk and knew how to keep ourselves safe. With all the sex we were having, we needed to know. The only sexual thing we pretty much stayed away from was anal as that was high risk, but we had done it a couple times using protection.

After a joint conversation with my doctor, Isaac made the decision one night to just not wear condoms anymore. It's not like he said, Ava I'm not strapping up anymore, he just didn't and when I finally noticed he informed me that he hadn't strapped up in over a month and a half. Oh, well damn. I wish I would have caught the clue a little earlier so I could have prepped myself with birth control because now I'm sitting on my patio missing the sunset for the first time because I'm too busy looking at a positive pregnancy test. I never once thought about getting pregnant and now it's like I had a new fear. What if my baby was born HIV positive? Would it be my fault? Oh God, how could I let this happen? Hearing my front door alarm alert that Isaac was coming in, I hid the test because I didn't want him to know until I talked to my doctor. I honestly wasn't even sure if I would keep the baby so there is no need right now to tell him.

When he walked on the patio, I smiled at how handsome he was. He had to cover a delivery shift today, so he was in his company's delivery uniform. He was sexy as hell and I wanted a special delivery.

"Hey, bae. How was your day?" he asked me before leaning

down and giving me his lips to kiss. I loved his lips; they were so soft.

"It was pretty mellow. Just laid around today." He pushed me over on the oversized lounge chair that he insisted we buy since he was now in my life.

Snuggling up under me, I scrunched my nose. "Eeeww. Go take a shower."

He lifted his arm and then sucked his teeth. "I don't even smell that bad, Ava. You got jokes."

He started tickling me and I burst into laughter. He was right, he didn't smell bad at all, but I just wanted to pick with him. I loved his touch and he knew that. I was a clingy girl-friend and I thought that would be a problem but it apparently wasn't because he was somewhat of a clingy boyfriend. We handle our business don't get me wrong, but we loved and cherished our time together.

He kissed my lips after he finished his tickle session. "You feel better, babe? You had me worried. I don't like you sick."

I had been sick for a few days, hence me even taking a pregnancy test to begin with. This is my first pregnancy, so I didn't know what to expect. Andre and I tried for years, but I never got pregnant. I wonder if this is why, because I was meant to have a baby with someone else.

"Yes, babe. I think it was the seafood I ate the other day." I got comfortable under him hoping he would change the subject. He just looked at me like he was thinking.

"Alright, let me jump in the shower since my girl thinks I stink and shit." He mushed my head lightly as he got up and I smacked his hand. He was always playing so much.

I made sure he was in the shower before I took the preg-nancy test from its hiding place and just looked at it. I was scared. I didn't want my baby to be positive, that would kill me. Anyone who knew me knew it was my dream to be a mother, but I never thought it was in the cards for me after being diagnosed. Seeing Marci with her children gave me hope but I never had the conversation with Isaac to even ascertain whether he wanted children and more importantly with me. It's one thing to be with me knowing I was HIV positive but a different thing to have a baby with me. If I was being one hundred percent honest with myself, I was enjoying Isaac while I could because I didn't think he was looking at us as a forever thing. I have a habit of setting myself up for the worst so the blow wouldn't hurt as much when it happens.

I took the pregnancy test inside the house and hid it and called my doctor to make an appointment. He only had an opening for the day after tomorrow, and I said that was fine. I needed to find out how far along I was and make the decision whether I was going to keep it or not.

֍

I WAS TIRED AS HELL AFTER WORK TODAY. MY CAMPAIGN was still going strong and I was so proud of that. I was happy I decided to take the day off tomorrow since I had my doctor's appointment. I wasn't sure if I was just tired, or this damn baby was making me tired, but I was done for tonight. All I wanted to do was go home, take a shower and go to bed. Isaac had inventory tonight, so I didn't expect him anytime soon. Opening my front door and walking in my house, I was so happy I took my clothes off at the damn door. I gave out an exaggerated sigh once they were all off. Walking deeper into my condo I decided I would get a bottled water and go on the patio, just bra and panties, to watch the sun set. I would take a shower after and go to bed. When I turned the corner, I almost jumped out of my damn skin seeing Isaac sitting at my breakfast nook in the kitchen.

"Isaac. Babe. What are you doing here? I thought you said

you had inventory?" I still had my hand over my chest, waiting for my heart to calm down. He looked up at me and I was confused by his facial expression. It wasn't an *I'm happy to see you* expression that I was used to. I looked at him with a confused face then focused my eyes on what was on the table in front of him.

Oh shit! How in the hell did he find that? I thought, no, I know I put it away. Damn him with his lurking ass.

"Ava, I did have inventory but I also have managers, so I don't have to be there. Yesterday, something was bothering me so I decided I would talk to you about it today. I thought I was overreacting in thinking you were pregnant but when you said that bullshit about the seafood making you sick, I knew something was up. As much damn seafood as you eat, I knew you was bullshitting me but I didn't understand why. That was until I was looking for something else and found this. Why were you hiding this, Ava? Were you gonna tell me?"

He was very calm in his tone, but I saw the anger behind his eyes. I didn't know if it was because I was pregnant and didn't tell him or because I was just pregnant.

I shifted on my feet and looked down at my hands. I was nervous and scared. "I wasn't really hiding it. I just didn't want you to see it yet."

His chuckle let me know he did not find my wordplay humorous. Hell, I knew I was grasping at straws. "Ava, don't fucking play with me. Why the fuck would you not want me to see this shit yet?"

He suddenly got quiet as if he was thinking then he raised to his feet and walked towards me. When he was directly in front of me, I looked up at him and he was looking at me with a look I had never seen.

"Were you planning to kill my fucking baby?"

"No! I...I don't know." I was so confused and scared.

"You don't know!" I jumped from the bass in his voice.

"I mean I was scared. We never talked about having a baby and I didn't know if you would want *me* to have your child." I backed up a little bit from him after I spoke.

"Why are you putting emphasis on *you*? Why the fuck wouldn't I want you to have my baby? I love you, I'm going to marry your little ass, so what the fuck?" Wait, what did he just say?

"You want to marry me?" He crossed his arms over his chest and just looked at me. I did the same because I didn't know what else to do.

"Ava, fuck yea...I'm going to marry your ass. What the fuck you thought?" He seemed to be upset at the fact that this wasn't knowledge I already knew, and it made me giggle a little bit.

"Isaac, why would I know that? We never talked about it. Why would I think you wanted to marry me and definitely have a baby with me? I'm HIV positive!" Now I was annoyed as hell.

Isaac stepped back and laughed hard. I was in my feelings about this laugh too. "We back on this HIV shit again? I thought we were past this stupid ass conversation. Ava, I am your damn man who fucks you unprotected knowing you are positive. Every fucking day I take a pill and just in case you didn't know I hate taking medication but I love you so I will do whatever I need to so we can be together and rock this shit out as normal as we can. I get tested every three months and do everything Doc Thomas tells me to so you sitting here mentioning that shit is an insult to my fucking intelligence."

I didn't know what to say, like I was literally speechless. We had a stare off and I could only think of one thing to muster. "I don't want my baby to be positive. I made an appointment for tomorrow with Dr. Thomas."

Isaac just looked at me. "What time?"

"It's at ten in the morning."

He stepped to me and kissed my lips. "I'll be there. Don't keep shit else from me, Ava Mae, or we gonna have a fucking problem. I'm going to pick up dinner so you can feed my baby."

With that, Isaac was out of the condo and I was there standing in my kitchen looking stupid as hell. He just put me in my place so smoothly, and although I felt like I should be mad, I was ironically turned on. I wonder if he's too mad to give me some dick tonight?

❦

I WAS NERVOUS ABOUT THE APPOINTMENT AND MAD THAT Isaac didn't touch me last night. I poked my ass out so hard on him and all he did was roll on his damn stomach. I was very mad. This morning, I think I'm doing something by waking him up with head and he lets me do a damn good job, then gets up like I didn't even do nothing. I haven't uttered a word to him since then and I don't care if I was being childish.

We were sitting in the waiting room waiting to be called back by Dr. Thomas. It didn't take long and when I went through the door, I didn't even try to hold it for Isaac causing him to chuckle. He moved close to me and wrapped his arms around me from the back to whisper in my ear.

"You mad I didn't give you any dick last night or this morning? I bet ya little ass won't keep shit else from me, Ava Mae Mills. Stop playing with me." He didn't even wait for my reaction as he released me from his hold with a smack to my ass and a laugh.

Oh, he thinks this is funny? See if I throw it back when he hitting it from the back next time. He wants to play, so can I. I sat across the room from Isaac. I felt his eyes on me, but I was not going to look at him. Hearing him laugh made me look at him and shoot daggers with my eyes at him. I can't stand him sometimes. Dr. Thomas didn't take long to come in and he immediately knew something was up.

"Hey, guys, what's going on? This is an unexpected visit." Dr. Thomas sat on his stool between us and looked at both of us with amused eyes.

I sat back in the chair and crossed my legs before shifting in my seat. Isaac chuckled, shaking his head before leaning forward in his seat resting his arms on his thighs.

"Doc, she pregnant and I had to find out on some sneaking shit so now she has an attitude because I wouldn't love on her." The expression on my face must have been priceless because Dr. Thomas looked at me and gave a hearty laugh.

I didn't find any of this funny and I was honestly scared. I mean, of course, I want children, but I honestly never thought I would have the opportunity, considering everything. This was new territory for me, hell, me being in a relationship is still new territory. I just wanted to make sure my baby would be okay. I don't understand what was so wrong about that. There is never anything wrong with wanting a healthy baby.

While they were having their own laughing session, I felt my emotions bubbling up and I decided to let them because I was tired. I was tired of everyone thinking my feelings were comical. I was not a joke and I didn't appreciate anyone treating me as such. Shooting up out of my seat, it was clear I caught them off guard.

"Since it's all a joke, the reason I didn't tell you is because I'm scared. I don't want to have a baby that's HIV positive because of me! So, yes! I wasn't going to tell you! I wanted to talk to my doctor first." I felt the tear, but I knocked it away.

Thirty Three

I saac

MY HEART WAS HURTING FOR THE FEAR THAT AVA HAS. I wanted to take all of her fears away because the fact was, I didn't have any. I had done the research around getting my babe pregnant when I decided to stop wearing protection. Dr. Thomas was now also my doctor with the sensitivity of my current lifestyle. I didn't want anyone talking negatively about me being with Ava considering her status, even my doctor.

Dr. Thomas sat up a little in his seat. "Ava, I apologize for my unprofessionalism in this situation. Why would you think your baby would be positive?"

She looked at him like he was crazy, and I had to chuckle at Bae. When Ava got a thought in her head it took an act of Congress to get it out. Crossing her arms over her chest and popping her now spreading hip out she looked at him with an air of annoyance.

"I have HIV! Duh!"

"Ava, just because you are positive does not automatically mean that your baby will be. You adhere to your ART and that is what is most important. You will continue to take it during your pregnancy and once the baby is born for four to six weeks the baby will receive a medicine called Zidovudine. It will protect your little one from any of the virus that is passed through the blood. We will test the baby fourteen to twenty-one days, one to two months, and four to six months of life. Ava, the odds of your baby being positive are extremely slim."

To that information from Dr. Thomas she sat down.

I could tell she was conflicted in her feelings and was still showing fear of the unknown. I had multiple conversations with my Uncle Mase and Aunt Marci about having a baby with Ava. They were living proof that you could have healthy babies and I wanted that with Ava and only Ava. I moved in front of her taking a squat position.

"Ava, babe." She looked at me with tears in her eyes. I reached up and placed her face in my hands before speaking. I love this woman more than I ever knew I could love. She came in my life and shook it up, but I needed it. "Our baby will be okay. This is a blessing and you, my wife, are going to have my baby."

She giggled and I knew it was because of me referring to her as my wife. That's who she was in my eyes and I also spoke things into existence, so as far as I'm concerned, she was Mrs. Mills. "OK, husband. I guess I'm having your baby."

I leaned up a bit and granted her the love of my lips. Hearing Dr. Thomas clear his throat let us know perhaps our kiss was getting intense.

"Our bad, Doc."

I stood before her and dug into my pocket retrieving a ring box. Watching her hold her breath made me smile inwardly. I had been holding on to this ring for about a month now. I knew she was what I wanted and needed, HIV and all. I turned the ring box around to reveal the marquise cut engagement ring I had custom made for her.

"Yes! Yes! Yes!" she shouted and jumped in my arms. I let my laughter overtake me because my babe was silly as fuck sometimes, but I wouldn't trade it for anything. She was my oasis in the desert.

"Damn, ma, you not even gonna let me ask you first?"

She pulled back and looked at me with tears falling down her cheeks. I smiled as I got on one knee.

"Ava Mae Boyd, everything you are was made just for me. Everything you have been through was necessary to get you to the point that you would be able to give me your love and I could give it back. My love for you is untainted as is God's love for the church. Will you bless me and not only be the mother of my children but my better half? Ava, will you marry me?" I slid the ring onto her finger and waited for her to tell me what I already knew.

"Yes, I will marry you, Isaac."

I smiled at her because I knew my babe. She wanted to jump up and down but she was trying to be reserved.

Hearing claps, I forgot Dr. Thomas was in the room with us still. I tend to zone out when it comes to Ava and nothing else matters.

"Congratulations you two! This is exciting news as is the new baby. Ava, I promise you, we will keep you healthy and your baby."

We both hugged Dr. Thomas before leaving with further instructions and scheduled appointments. Ava's gynecologist worked in tandem with Dr. Thomas so she would have to see him next. I was excited about having my first child and I knew it was a blessing.

"DAMN, MAN! WELCOME TO THE DADDY CLUB, MY NIGGA." Anthony was just as excited as I was about my new chapter in life. Ava was sixteen weeks pregnant now and we were going to find out what we were having. Ava looked sexy as fuck carrying my baby. With her being HIV positive she was a worrywart, so we stayed in the doctor's office to appease her nerves. She was still adhering to her ART and I to my PrEP.

"Thank you! I can't wait to give her my last damn name. I need that to happen before she has my kid though. She wants a wedding and I'm not going to take that away from her. I told her ass she got a month to plan it and we walking down somebody's aisle." I laughed at myself because Ava's little ass almost cursed me out when I told her that but I bet her ass planning.

Anthony was holding his son Max to his chest while he slept. I couldn't wait to have that type of love. Max was all Anthony talked about these days and I was happy for him. After he and Sis lost their first, I never thought he would bounce back. He was in a bad ass depression which was hard because so was Myah. They were both going through it but look at them now. Our Man Time Sunday was now spent with his little one and I wasn't mad in the least because soon this would be me.

Ava and Myah were out spending our damn money and I knew my black card was smoking because every time a purchase is made, I get a text alert. Well, let's just say, my texts have been popping all damn day. I didn't give a fuck though, especially since I had convinced Ava to move into my house and sublease her condo. I had to promise her she could redecorate, and I have been paying for it for three weeks now. She enlisted Tae Smith Designs for the job and when I tell you I was lowkey in awe of the transformation my house was going through, I was. I guess it was true what they said... A woman can turn a house into a home.

"Bruh, Ava ass about to be bent the hell over all night with all this money she spending."

Anthony's laughter was so hard and loud it stirred Max out of his sleep. He shuffled in Anthony's arms, but the rocking put him back to sleep.

Just as I was about to speak, I heard the alarm in the house announcing Myah's entry which I knew meant Ava was behind her. I watched the door to the mancave waiting for my babe to come through and when she did, I couldn't even hide my smile. Ava pregnant was a gorgeous sight. Her little baby bump fit her and it damn sure fit me with her. We made eye contact and like a magnet, she came to me. When she sat next to me, I pulled her into me, placing my hand on her stomach and kissing her temple.

"Hey, babe. How was your day?"

I looked at her with an arched brow. "I need to be asking you. Spending money like Floyd Mayweather." I gave a chuckle with my statement, but she didn't seem amused.

"Well, I could always take the wedding dress back that I bought for next weekend. Oh, and cancel the venue." She tried to get up from her seat, but I stopped her before she could.

"Next weekend? Wait you're ready?" I was trying to stifle my excitement because I was more than ready to marry her. Ava made it clear that she wanted a wedding, but she also let it be known she wanted something small and intimate.

With the smile that I fell in love with shining on her face, she kissed my lips. "I've been ready, I just wanted to get everything in place."

"Ava, how the hell we gonna get married next weekend? Don't you have to send invitations or some shit?" I was confused about how she was pulling this together so quickly. I wasn't mad but I just wanted to make sure she was going to have what she wanted.

"Isaac, I did electronic invitations and I already got RSVPs. It's only our immediate family and the people you had on your list." I nodded my head because I didn't think about electronic invitations. I was just happy that after next weekend she would have my name. We had gotten our marriage license last week, so we were ready.

"Well, you got everything planned, ma. Just tell me what I need to wear and where I need to be. I'm ready to make you a Mills." I kissed her lips before she could say anything.

We sat around for maybe two more hours then we made our way home. I loved having Ava as a part of my home life now because she was the most important part of it. We talked about the wedding that would be happening the next weekend. My baby had already spoken to my tailor and he had my suit. I received an email from him with a fitting appointment for Wednesday and all I could do was smile because my babe seemed to have thought of everything. Throughout the night, I received text messages from those Ava had sent invitations to that were on my list. They were excited about the weekend and I couldn't help but admit, so was I. In six days, my Ava would be a Mills.

Epilogue

The Wedding Day
Isaac

"ISAAC, BABE!" HEARING AVA CALL MY NAME IN ECSTASY was the perfect way to start our wedding day. Sure, we weren't even supposed to see each other right now but I needed her. I hadn't seen her since Thursday morning when she left our home with Myah's annoying ass. Talking about you can't see her until she is walking down the aisle. Bullshit! Who's going to stop me from seeing my pregnant fiancée? Not no one!

That's why I have her ass bent over in this bathroom at our wedding venue. My baby picked this dope spot uptown Charlotte, Skyline Terrace, to have our intimate ceremony and reception. I'm sure her people are looking for her because I snatched her little ass up when she was walking past the bathroom in the hallway between our suites. She just got her makeup finished and still had on her "Bride" robe. I was tearing her ass up too. I felt lowkey bad, but this pregnant pussy is the devil.

"Bae, be quiet before we get caught." Her laughing made

me laugh and break my stroke concentration. Feeling her walls clamp down on my shit, I knew it was a wrap.

Releasing myself into her I leaned back slightly. It was hard as hell hitting it from the back and not pulling her hair that had grown out. I loved that shit and so did she. I pulled out of her and told her not to move. I took my time cleaning her before letting her stand upright. She was so beautiful, and I appreciated her makeup being natural.

"Isaac, you aren't supposed to see me." I laughed at her faux attitude with me because she knew she wanted to see me just as bad. Her ass had been texting me all damn night about doing this.

"Ava, stop playing with me. You know I need to see you daily. Fuck outta here, ma." I smacked her ass as I walked past her to the door. Feeling her hit me on my back with a giggle, I pulled the bathroom door open.

"Y'all some nasty, impatient fukas." Anthony and Myah were standing outside of the door, looking at us like parents who just caught us fucking. Well, technically, we were, but yeah.

Looking at Ava, she actually looked shamed and that made me laugh. I didn't even want to address it, so I simply kissed her lips and walked to my suite to finish my preparation to meet her down the aisle. Anthony wasn't far behind my stride as I entered my suite. I wasn't sure why we needed a whole suite when it was literally just me and Anthony in the wedding, but bae said the suites came with the package.

"You ready, man?" I took a sip of my water and looked at Anthony with a smirk. This was my boy and we had been through a lot of shit together. I wouldn't change any of it.

"Man, I been ready to marry her little ass." We laughed at my statement and dapped each other.

"Bruh, I have to tell you. I'm so fucking proud of you. You are taking on something that I don't even know if I could. I love Ava and trust me, I don't judge her, but let's be real, man. This is heavy. You altered the way you moved to love her correctly and I respect that shit."

Anthony saying that meant a lot. I never needed or sought his approval of my decision to be with Ava, but having it meant a lot.

We talked for a bit and then my Father and Uncle came through for a toast and a prayer. I was ready to marry my one and I was not now or will I ever be ashamed to love her. We all have our cross to bear and as her soon to be husband, I am willingly going to bear it with her. Love is free but the labor cost behind it is a bitch.

AVA

"I can't believe your hot ass was in the damn bathroom getting dicked down not even an hour before you walk down the aisle." I couldn't stop laughing at Myah as she scolded me like a child for having sex with my fiancé.

"Myah! You act like I was having sex with someone other than Isaac. Hell, he pulled me into the bathroom. I just wanted to get the nervousness out of both of our systems." I said that with a seemingly straight face, but Myah's facial expression evoked laughter.

I was so excited that in less than an hour I would be walking down the aisle to become Mrs. Isaac Mills. Never in a million years would I think anyone would want me much more marry me and have a baby with me. I thought my life was over when I got my diagnosis, but God clearly saw otherwise. He brought me Isaac and I am forever grateful. Looking at myself in the mirror as the Myah zips up my wedding dress, I can't believe I'm here again. Marrying the love of my life. Andre was my everything and most would think that I hate him, but I simply couldn't. I don't for one second doubt the love he had for me, even in the mistake he made. It just goes to show that one bad decision can change your life and the others around you. He would always have a piece of my heart and Isaac was okay with that.

It will never be lost to me the sacrifice that Isaac makes daily to be with me. I mean, he is basically taking a one a day pill for the rest of his life to be with me. He gets tested every three months and even switched his doctor to mine. If the man never verbally told me he loves me ever again, his actions daily screamed it. Three weeks ago, I accidentally cut myself and he didn't shy away from me. That was a major reaction change from the dinner we all had months earlier. He no longer had a fear of my blood. Feeling our daughter kick around in me was the best feeling ever. Yes, we were having a little girl. We found out Wednesday and the fear in Isaac's eyes was real. It made me laugh because he swore the Lord was cursing him. Anthony told him not to worry though because he was going to train Lil' Max to be her guard dog. Me and Myah could not stop laughing as these fools actually sat down writing out a plan for it. They had a "Big Cuz" training schedule for Max. I promise this schedule was not to be taken lightly either as Isaac harassed my nerves for a whole day about how I "fit" into this plan.

"Are you ready, baby girl?" Hearing my father's voice brought me out of my thoughts. I love my father more than anything. I wasn't what you call a daddy's girl per se, but I loved my father deeply. When I was diagnosed, he tried to come to the hospital and kill Andre before the Lord could take him.

"I'm ready, Daddy. Do I look pretty?" I wanted validation because what girl doesn't want her daddy to tell her she's pretty?

"Baby girl, you are the prettiest girl I have ever seen. From the day you popped out of your mama, I knew you were gonna give me hell. From the sandbox, you had little niggas on your ass, and I was trying to make them swallow dirt. Of course, your mama told me I couldn't, but I tried on a couple of them little crumb snatchers."

I couldn't stop laughing at my Dad.

A single forehead kiss was all I needed to calm my nerves from my father. Before getting dressed I looked at the wedding rooftop venue and it was laid out beautifully. It was already set up in a reception-style with tables and things, with an aisle down the middle for us to walk down. It was only Myah by my side and Anthony by Isaac's. Mama Mills did my hair and I absolutely loved it. It had grown out a lot from when I cut it, so I started letting her do my hair about a month and a half ago. My parents didn't live close, so I definitely welcomed the motherly figure close by. As we walked down the hall with Myah holding my train, I begin to get nervous.

What if in a year or two he realizes he made a mistake marrying me? I mean, I have HIV, why would anyone want to be with someone like me?

The thought alone made me halt my steps. "I can't do this."

Myah rushed in front of me and looked me in my eyes. "What the hell you mean you can't do this, Ava?"

My father was now looking intently at me and as if he could read my mind he spoke to my insecurity. "Ava, baby. You are worth it. All the sacrifice he is making to be with you. Taking meds for the rest of his life, getting checked often, baby. He does it because he loves you. First Corinthians, chapter thirteen, verses four through eight tell you exactly what love is. Isaac has shown that love in every way. He has shown you Agape love, baby."

I heard my father, but I was still doubtful. All the fear I had at the beginning of our courtship made me want to run.

Myah was like the other half of my brain so she must have known because she turned and ran out onto the rooftop. I wasn't sure what she was doing but I had my suspicions.

"Daddy, I just need a minute. I'm gonna go in the room and sit down for a second." I didn't wait for a response as I turned to make my escape.

Halfway down the hallway the next voice I heard made me stop and take a breath. "Ava! Where are you going, ma?"

I couldn't turn around, I just couldn't. I was scared of what I would see. In true Isaac fashion, I didn't have to turn around because before I could form my next thought, he was standing in front of me looking more handsome than I had ever seen. Damn. This man is fine as hell and I know he could have any woman he wants. Why the hell would he want to be with me?

In a low but stern tone, Isaac spoke. "Ava, you gonna leave me at the altar now? Let me find out I'm trying to marry Julia Roberts and no one told me."

That got a laugh out of me because I love Julia Roberts and I made him binge-watch all of her movies one weekend. He took a special interest in *Runaway Bride*. He would not stop talking about that movie so this whole scene was ironic. When I finally looked back at him after my laughter, he still held a stoic look and I just needed to know why.

"Isaac, why me? You could have any healthy girl you want. I mean you fine as hell and the dick... I just don't get it." He chuckled at my statement. I'm sure it was the dick comment but hell this man has me climbing walls often and that's before I get the dick. When I get the dick, I often think I'm in an alternate reality it feels so good.

He moved in closer to me then placed his hands on my face forcing me to look him in the eyes. "Because you own my heart. I love you, Ava, and my love doesn't see a girl with HIV My love sees Ava the girl God made just for me. Your status was just a spice in our love recipe but that doesn't make our recipe any less appetizing to me, baby. You're carrying my daughter. I want you to later carry my son. You are everything I'm not and for that, I respect you. I respect you for your strengths, but I love you for your weaknesses."

I was officially through and needed my makeup redone. It's as if he took those words straight from God's mouth because it was the exact confirmation I needed from God. I had prayed about this and I was nervous because I felt like I didn't have an answer but now I was answered, and boldly. I wrapped my arms around him and held him tight. This man was going to be my husband, father of my children, and I was going to be his wife. I had never been so proud in my life.

"Can we go get married now, baby, or we gonna stand out here and just hug on each other? A nigga hungry and I want to eat." I couldn't stop my laughter and I heard Myah and Anthony laughing too.

"Yes, baby, I can't wait to be Mrs. Mills. Let's go." He gave me a quick kiss then handed me off to Myah.

Myah rushed me back to the room where my makeup was touched up and then everything was reset. That day, I married the love of my life and I felt like the luckiest girl in the world. During our reception it was sunny and nice then all of a sudden, a torrential downpour happened out of nowhere. As soon as it started it was over and the sun was back out. I looked up at the sky wondering what the hell was going on and that's when I saw it. A rainbow.

YEAR 2012

"Ava, baby, I'm so sorry I did this to you." Andre had been apologizing since we both found out he had full-blown AIDS and I was HIV positive.

I was hurt and disappointed. When I first found out I was in disbelief but that soon changed when I saw him on his death bed. He hadn't taken care of himself and now it was too late. He hated doctors so he rarely went. There was no early detection, so a cold had turned into pneumonia and now the doctors said it was any day now.

"Andre, stop! Stop apologizing because I forgive you. I know you didn't do this on purpose. I just hate that this is going to take you away from me. What am I going to do without you? No one will ever love me with this."

My emotions wouldn't let me be great and the tears were automatic.

Feeling Andre tighten his hold on my hand made me give my attention to him. For the past couple of days, he hasn't been strong enough to do anything so him doing that mean a lot.

"Ava, you will I promise you. Someone will love you past that. I didn't ruin you and I'm so sorry if you think I did. I love you with everything in me and I'll die a thousand deaths for your happiness. You will find him and when you do you will know it will be true because I will be there. Just look for the rainbow in the sky."

❦

MY RAINBOW IN THE SKY. EVERYONE WAS LOOKING AT IT because it was literally right over me and Isaac. The photographer even posed us under it because he just couldn't believe how beautiful and vibrant it was and right over us. So here I stand, arms wrapped around my husband looking in his eyes as he looks down at me. I'm standing under the love of my present and the love of my past with a love of my future in my womb. I stood on my tiptoes to give Isaac my lips, hearing the camera shutters I knew this moment was being recorded.

It was at that moment, I knew this would undoubtedly be my favorite picture of them all.

Even in a situation such as ours, there was one thing for certain and two things for sure: our love was untainted from day one.

The End

AFTERWORD

A Letter from A Reader:

When I learned about Mel Dau's new storyline, I was both
excited and afraid... excited that an author would be so bold
to write a love story where the main character was HIV
positive, and afraid that it wouldn't be authentic and
accurate. So many other authors have written about the
condition, making the person with it the villain, trying to
hurt others, or a bad girl being punished for promiscuous
behavior. Almost always, it ends up with the affected
character succumbing to a quick and painful death, or being
submitted to a life all alone and full of shame. But these
stories are far from what the majority of people that live with
this condition experience every day.

Let me be clear, this disease can be deadly. For those that
choose to ignore the signs, get tested and seek treatment,
death will soon follow. However, life with HIV can be a
healthy one. And with the proper regimen, people are able to
live fully normal lives and love without fear of passing on the

condition. They can even have children – healthy ones – and can even breastfeed those children without subjecting them to danger. Research has found that a person who has been diagnosed and adhering to proper treatment now has a normal lifespan. It doesn't have to be a killer disease. But my people are so afraid of the stigma that they refuse to get tested.

I have lived with this disease for the last fifteen years, and the worst part is that people no longer see you as worthy. More than anything, I want someone to love me because, and not in spite of. I had a man that married me in spite of, and he reminded me of that constantly throughout our marriage. We eventually divorced, and my biggest fear was never finding anyone else that would want me. I didn't even tell my best friend until ten years after my diagnosis because I was afraid of the stigma and the rejection. Although I have been undetectable for years and am in good health, I know that people are afraid, and for that reason, I closed myself off from love completely. By writing this book, Mel Dau is bringing awareness so that maybe one day, I can find someone who doesn't see my disease.

Mel Dau, thank you so much for taking on this topic. Thanks for consulting a person actually living with this disease to make sure you have an accurate depiction. Thanks for revealing the truth, and thank you for showing that even those that suffer from this disease deserve love and compassion. Even with HIV, true love is untainted.

Your devoted reader.